CLINGING TO THE EDGE

CLINGING
to the
EDGE

short stories

THERESA RIVERA

PORTLAND • OREGON
INKWATERPRESS.COM

Publisher: Inkwater Press | www.inkwaterpress.com

ISBN-13 978-1-62901-623-8 | ISBN-10 1-62901-623-3

1 3 5 7 9 10 8 6 4 2

To my children, Christina, Michael and James. Each one of you are my favorite child. I'm so grateful to be your mom.

To my readers, I know you get scared and tired and overwhelmed. You're not alone and don't give up. There are quiet, tender, comical, poignant, kind reminders that you are loved without question and cherished. It's all there if you are patient and can take the time to notice the interesting nuances of loveliness and mystery whispering around the corners. You've got this.

Table of Contents

The Ghost Tamer

I FIRST BECAME AWARE OF HER THE DAY WE LOOKED AT THE house before we signed the final papers. She was pale, thin, and lurked about the stairwell. I even saw her briefly the day we moved in. She was staring at the children. I wondered if we'd made a mistake. When she became aware that I was watching her around my kids, she moved soundlessly out the window.

A few weeks later, we were more or less settled into our two-story, turn-of-the-century home. It sat on a flat landscape surrounded by a barn and stables, a former carriage house, and several out-buildings. A more recent addition to the property had been the horse barn, which were surrounded by a training corral and several holding pens. Inside the barn were my own mare and three others. We also owned two geldings and were hoping to raise and sell other horses for racing or rodeos.

One evening after unpacking until late in the kitchen, I had left a box of aluminum pans on the counter. In the dark of midnight, there was an abrupt clattering, followed by the frightened screams of our kids … I think.

I went down to the kitchen, shaking with fright, while Les soothed Adam and Tamra Blue. I put the pans away and felt my pulse return to normal.

Just as I shut off the lights in the kitchen, I saw her weeping on the porch. Her long hair was draped over her arms and she sat huddled in a corner. I could hear soft crying sounds, but maybe that was just Tamra Blue, who was still a little shaken.

I suppose I should've been scared, but there was something about the way the poor thing hovered there on that chilly porch. And, anyway, I had confronted her kind before. It began when I was a child. I had watched as my grandmother danced gracefully around the coffin that held her crippled remains after she had died. She had been a dancing showgirl in her young life, something her daughter (yes, my very pretentious mother) had been embarrassed about.

Gram's gray hair had gone back to its original ebony color, and it rippled down her back as her slippered feet twirled her around and around.

At the end of the Mass, she gave me a wink, and then she was gone. Later, when I had tried to tell my grieving mother what I had seen, she became furious at me and tried to abolish such nonsense with a sound slap across my face.

After that, I thought it best to keep my visions of the unknown world to myself. Not many people were very comfortable with the idea of death in the first place. It was very fashionable for the movie industry to idealize ghosts or souls or what have you. It was also part of the culture to sweep anything that can't be explained scientifically into the cracks of the technology floorboards.

When I was in college, I would see a man who rode the subway all day every day. He seemed to ride many of the same routes as me. His skin was tinged yellow; he had deep, dark eyes with no real expression in them. He wore an army green coat that went almost to the ground. His hair was brown, and he had a small, sensitive mouth that never spoke or smiled. He carried with him, always, a ragged photograph of an unknown sub-ject. I wondered sometimes if he was still riding those trains.

So when I saw the tall, lithe form of the young woman in the house, it had not surprised or con-cerned me.

Something about her seemed far too vulner-able to be alarming, so I went out and sat next to her. I even tried to put my arm around her, but it only surrounded the cold air where I thought her shoulders were. I unconsciously wanted to stroke her hair from her face, but, again, my fingers only passed through the image.

I tried to talk to her.

"Please tell me who you are." But when I spoke, she flashed her stark face at me in surprise and left. She ran off the porch, past the barns and corrals, like a white dove flying through the night.

I let her go.

I was suddenly exhausted.

The next morning, I told Les about her over coffee. He put his cup down and stared at me. He tried to put a joke in his voice, but it was no good. Eyes tell everything.

"Oh, knock it off, Jo! You're pulling my leg."

"No, Les, I'm not." I looked right at him and kept my voice calm. "She's been around since before we got here. They don't just come from nowhere, you know."

Les tapped his cup with his fingernails, making little tinkling sounds. Then he heaved a windy sigh. I could smell the coffee and cigarettes on his breath from across the table.

"Josephine, maybe we need to call Dr. Silverstein. Maybe you're just plumb tired from all this moving 'round. You need some rest. 'Sides, the medication you're on, those brochures say it can make you feel a little funny in the head."

"I've already been diagnosed as being funny in the head, Les. Remember those nice nurses from that hospital? I know they didn't spend those six weeks asking me all those wily questions for nothing. After all, the insurance company paid for my degree in PTSD that I earned, but this isn't about that."

I was trying to be funny, sort of.

It was actually true.

The doctors told me that delusions could be associated with post-traumatic stress disorder. I wasn't so sure.

Les patted my hand. I noticed his wedding ring was tightly embedded in his finger. During the years, his finger had grown around it, all comfortable and as if it was part of him. Loyal Les. That's what I thought of him as. When we'd been married ten years ago, he'd been skinny as a rail. A rodeo rider. Son of a Montana rancher. An artist. A far cry from city slicker me. He loved me. Mostly. Though, I knew I'd given him a run for his money over the years.

"I want you to take 'er easy today. There ain't nothin' gotta be done today that can't wait. Once the kids are on that bus, you lie back. I'm goin' to the shop and work on some designs."

He took a last sip of his black coffee and he stood, pulling up his jeans underneath his expanding belly. The belt buckle always looked like it should hurt, the way it stuck there underneath his chub, but he never said so. He took a long drag of his cigarette. I didn't like that he smoked in the house in the mornings. I would grab the Lysol and crack the window after he left.

"Oh well."

He probably didn't like that I had PTSD and

had nearly broken us up last year with my bizarre behavior making the headlines back in Boston

He would grab his heart and hold on tight.

People learned to give in to the large stuff sometimes in a marriage. It was the damned lost toothpaste caps that caused the real problems.

Adam was trying on his masculinity these days. At nine he was getting tall, like me. He was gangly and would have large hands. He didn't want or need my help getting ready for school. Tamra Blue, on the other hand, liked me to braid her hair in neat, straight braids. She had the most beautiful blue eyes and her hair was ash blonde. Both Les and I had black hair. But Tamra Blue had inherited an off color from some long-ago grandmother or aunt.

It irritated my mother that I named my daughter after a color. But blue was my favorite color, and Tamra's eyes were blue. Mother said all babies' eyes were blue at birth, and she wondered how I could tell that they weren't going to be brown or green like mine or Les's. It drove my mother crazy that I was always right. (One of the joys of my life.)

"Sounds like something you'd call one of your horses too!" she'd snapped irately. She didn't understand that to a horse lover that was a compliment.

I kissed my kids goodbye and smelled the scent of tempera paints that seem to permeate their coats from school. Their lunches were packed with carrot sticks, apples, and peanut butter smooshed between bread slices. I cut the big, thick slices from the bread I made with my machine.

My mare, Ashleigh's Grace, huffed gray snorts of air as she watched me stare after the big yellow bus as it trundled down the lane. Her body was with foal, her coat was shiny, and her flanks were plump. She had waited patiently until now for me to come give her some oats and run the curry brush over her.

I knew Les told me to rest, but Ashleigh was my soulmate, so I'd take care of her first. I tromped to the barn in my muck boots. The clomping of my feet left a trail of ghostly footprints in the white-diamond ground cover of the early winter snow. I didn't miss the connection.

The hard frost that had preceded the snow had given us a short fall that now was every bit a promise of the cold winter that we were in for. The morning air was so pure and wonderful. Closer to the barns, the clarity of it turned into the smell of horseshit and straw. This to me was purely an aphrodisiac. This wasn't the city.

Les and I moved there because he wanted to come home. The doctor told me I needed peace and advised me to kick back and try a new lifestyle. Also, me making the headlines back in Boston after what had happened made me somewhat popular in way that wasn't particularly flattering. There in Montana I was just Josephine Porter, wife of the artist Les Porter and mother of two. This lifestyle was more inclined to handle my erratic mood swings. Dr. Silverstein said he was glad that I would have the chance to get in touch with the things that I found most comforting and stable.

So there I was, standing next to the stable.

Ashleigh put her warm nose on my neck. It felt great. I spoke soothingly. The little foal's body quaked inside hers. She grunted a little in surprise at the movement. We looked into each other's eyes. Horses had such wonderful eyes. Large and brown, deep like their souls.

As suddenly as the pans had dropped to the floor last night, Ashleigh bolted her head around in startlement. When she did this, her jaw mashed my lips against my teeth. "Damnit!" I shrieked in pain. She looked behind her wildly, like something had bitten her flank. I tasted blood and felt a lump beginning to form in the corner of my mouth.

I couldn't see what had startled Ashleigh. I was looking around, but I thought I knew what might have frightened her.

"It's alright, Ashleigh. She's just a little lost or something. Don't worry about it." I dabbed at the blood on my face as it ran warmly down my cool chin. I filled her pail with some oats and checked her water. "I'll be out a little later, sweetheart." I patted her neck and she was calmer. I was starting to feel nauseous.

The meds did that.

As I headed back to the house, I listened to the silent air. There were sparkly little crystals

Clinging to the Edge

floating in the sunlight. The air was so cold its tears shined.

I did rest that day, and for the next three. That was just the way it went for me sometimes. Les was so good. So kind. He made dinner for the kids and sent them into our room at night so I could help them with their homework. "School smarts is your mom's department," he always drawled to them in his leathery voice. "If you want to know the practical stuff, com'n see me then," he teased.

Les and me. How we ever got together was pure providence. He was as fascinated by my polished law degree and upper-crust background as I was about his Western charm and improper grammar. "A back wood's fortune seeker." I believe that's what my proper Bostonian mother had called him.

Les was an artist. That's how we met. He designed saddles and painted horse pictures. I'd gone to a flea market to find something for my new apartment, with its clean, white walls, and fell in love with one of his paintings, which was on display in the Western section. I loved horses. I'd spent a great deal of my youth in the classic black habits my mother made me wear when I took my Saturday riding lessons. Guess I was lucky that was the only habit she made me wear. The time she'd found me in the hay having sex with one of the stable hands when I was fifteen had her calling all the private Catholic girls' schools on the East Coast. Her punishment was my escape. Hurray!

But she made sure I never got near a horse again. Until I met Les, I had put the love away.

I bought his horse painting and in the transaction ended up asking him out. He was surprised at my forwardness, but he accepted. Through contacts in my law firm, I eventually set him up with an art dealer who liked to sell Western themed art items to New Yorkers and Japanese businessmen. Les's genius made him rich. It really pissed my mom off, which was why I asked him to marry me. That and the fact that I loved him .... and I was pregnant with Adam.

When I got up the evening of the third night, the sun was just setting behind the Red Lodge Mountains. There were clouds gathering around their tips, so the whole sky was cotton-candy pink with clouds. This was the area where Les had grown up. I loved it almost from the moment I arrived there.

There was something about the landscape, the way it rolled along in colors of ocean green with gentle hills that rose and fell like breasts. The mountains to the west were called the Beartooth Mountains. They were blue against the twilight. In the winter, there were long strips of snow that streaked down the front of them, evidence of a thriving ski resort not far from town. We bought this old ranch with its wonderful house, which sat in the middle of the property like a grand old lady who would not be ignored. In front of the gate, there was a quiet road that led east to Red Lodge or farther on to Billings.

The house came complete with wonderfully deep corners and closets, oddly shaped windows, banisters that gleamed after polishing, and smoothly worn hardwood floors. It made little difference to me that it had also come with its own ghost. What queenly house, or woman for that matter, should not have a little secret or two?

New houses, with their youthful shine and cedar decks, could not boast such amenities. I felt so safe here. One look and I knew it would be the place to raise kids and ride horses. I was home.

Les came ambling out of his saddle shop. He still made my heart dance with his easy good looks. He had thick, wavy black hair salted a little with gray. He stepped up to the balustrade of the porch and gave my cheek a kiss. He lit one last cigarette before he went in the house. His fingers were stained with leather oil and his cheeks were also smudged with it. He'd also had a drink or two. The smell of him was brought to me on the little afternoon breeze, like a scented, airy baptism as it wafted gently over me.

"Feelin' better, cowgirl?" The end of the cigarette was glowing like the eye of the devil as the light shifted.

"Yep. I think I'll get cleaned up and make some dinner."

Just then, Tamra Blue came around the house

screaming hysterically, tears streaming down her face, scraggly braids flying behind her pink ears.

"Tamra Blue, what's the matter? And where is your hat?" I hollered.

She was so mad. "Talk to Adam! He filled my hat full of horse turds, and when I put it on, they spilled all over me!" If she'd had claws, they would have been out. For a moment, I could almost see them, all shiny, long, and silver, covered in Adam's blood. My youngest child ran to me and buried her head in my hip.

Les was trying not to laugh. I guess growing up on a ranch and being a big brother himself, he could appreciate the joke. I gave him a look and said, "Come on, Tam; it's time for dinner." A moment later, I heard Les calling for Adam in a tone that meant business.

I showered and made dinner. After dinner, I did the dishes. Then I decided to polish some old candlesticks I'd found at an estate sale once. After that, I decided to make cookies for Adam and Tamra Blue's class Halloween parties. I made dozens. I cut them all out, spread orange frosting over them, and put little faces on them with candy corn. Then I waxed the hardwood floor in the formal dining room. At about 3:00 a.m., Les wandered downstairs in his bathrobe, his hair standing on end and his chin fuzzy with a dark beard shadow. He looked at me but didn't say anything. He knew me. He knew the routine. A few days down and then the endless activity for several days. He didn't bother to ask if I was coming to bed.

I went out on the porch because my face was hot from working and scrubbing the floor so vivaciously. The air was bursting with cold and enveloped me with its chilly arm. The moon was moving in its silent walk through the clouds. It casts shadows in small glances here and there on the ground. I saw her during one of those moments. She was staring back at me all vacant-eyed and gaunt, like they did sometimes. I took another deep breath and bid her softly, "Come here. I won't hurt you."

She just stood there. I didn't know if she could hear me. I sat down on the porch. It was one those quiet moments when it all snuck up on me and I wondered what it was all about. My teeth began to chatter a little. She was still standing there, but then, suddenly, she was nearer the porch. One of Les's cigarette lighters had been dropped on the step, and I picked it up and began to play with it. I started flicking it just enough to send tiny little sparks out. I felt her come a little closer. I let one flame escape and there she was, standing right in front of me. I tried to stay calm, but my heart was thumping pretty hard. Soundlessly, a white hand ran its fingers through the flame. I was too chicken to look at her face.

"Can you hear me?" I said in a trembling whisper.

And then her rage erupted. Her body seemed to snap like the flame and flew up to the naked tree. The wind began to shriek. She opened her mouth and wailed. Her eyes seemed to roll back in her head. It was hideous. I was scared shitless as I jumped up, ran, and then flattened myself against the door when I got inside.

Les came running down the stairs; he pulled me to his sturdy chest.

"It's alright, baby. I promise. Shhh, you'll wake the kids."

I stopped screaming. Or else she did. Either way, it was silent again.

The next morning, Les called Dr. Silverstein in Boston and received the name of a counselor in Billings. Her name was Lola Kicking Horse. I liked that she had the word "horse" in her name.

On a morning soon after, the kids left for school, we drove the hour or so from our Red Lodge ranch to the city. Or what constituted a city in a state like Montana. We passed through Laurel and the smell of the oil refinery grabbed our lungs and filled them.

Lola Kicking Horse greeted me warmly. There were some folks I instantly liked. They had a great presence. She reminded me of a warm brown blanket. Brown because her skin was sort of a milky umber. Her eyes were so dark and deep I wondered if they could ever shine. Her high cheek bones and flat nose gave her an exotic, almost tropical look. She had a low forehead from which her inky black hair was parted, and she had her hair braided in classically thick, impossibly neat braids.

She was a textbook example of all the pictures of Native American women I'd seen. I was smitten by her beauty and knew my classic white-woman looks were small in comparison to the texture and depth of hers. She offered me juice or tea. I opted for the tea.

We sat on comfortable couches across a colorful rug from each other.

"Dr. Silverstein faxed me some of your file today, Mrs. Porter, or do you prefer Josephine?"

"I like Jo."

"Alright," she said, "Jo it is. Dr. Silverstein and I go way back, believe it or not. We went to undergrad school together. We were great friends."

It was hard for me to imagine the prim but kindly Jewish doctor from Boston and this earthy brown woman in a relationship. But, hey, I was there because I was seeing a ghost at my house, so who was I to judge relationship?

We spent several minutes in chitchat, with her reminding me about the rules of confidence. How she wouldn't reveal anything I said unless she thought I might harm myself or someone else. I'd heard it all before and, being a former attorney, knew my rights and her obligations anyway.

We talked. She asked me questions. I answered.

Finally, she asked me about the ghost.

What I loved best about counselors was that they asked all about being crazy as if they were asking what I thought of sightseeing in Ireland or gardening.

I shrugged my shoulders. "Not much to tell," I

said. "She's just hanging around my house like she's been there awhile. I feel sorry for her in a way."

"Really," Lola said. "Tell me why you feel sorry for her."

Actually, I was surprised to be asked this. Usually, Dr. Silverstein and the others would look at me after an admission like this and say, "How are your sleep habits?" or, "What are your drug habits?" and so forth. My answer would be something crass like, "I can't get into either of those habits, especially sleep. I hear it's highly addictive."

I looked Lola full in the eyes to see if she was being serious. She was looking back, just waiting for my answer. *People are a lot different here in Montana*, I thought.

"Well … she seems so … lost. She's always crying, shrieking, or running off. Maybe she is scared of something. Maybe I scare her. I tend to be pretty intimidating, you know."

Lola sat with her chin perched atop her thumb and index finger and smiled slightly at my remark about intimidation.

"How are you intimidating?" she asked.

"I'm really just kidding. Maybe she senses I used to be a lawyer and that I went bat shit and had to quit. But, seriously, she is just there at our house, and she's been there since before we moved in."

"Tell me why you think she is sad or lost."

"Well, we've only just met, her and I; it's a little over-personal for me to ask those questions yet."

I couldn't help trying to be funny. It really messed with these clinical heads.

Lola looked amused and jotted comments down on her pad.

"Why are you trying to make fun of yourself?" she asked next.

Well, that was a new one for me. Usually, at this point they just handed over the prescription or told me I needed to check in to the local mental health unit. I was a little stumped. She wasn't going to let me off that easy.

"Well," I said, "I guess humor is a way of accepting that I'm a little, you know ..."

"What?" she said quietly "You're a little what?"

"Well, post-traumatic, loony tunes, maniacally inclined, crazy."

She studied me a minute. Made a few more notes and said, "Well, humor is a great buffer to many things that would otherwise be too painful to deal with. I think it's okay to use humor to deal with things. But let's get back to your ghost. Tell me more about her."

We talked for well over the allotted hour's time. "It was a pleasure to meet you, Jo," she said warmly as she ushered me out of her office to the reception desk, where I made my next appointment. She squeezed my hand before I left. "Everything is alright, Jo." I don't know why, but I felt like crying.

I walked out of the office, and Les was waiting in our Suburban. He was reading the paper. I hopped in. He started the engine and said, "I need to go see Carson about having those saddles shipped. I'll be going up town. Would you like to come with me or should I drop you off so you can get some lunch and do so some shopping?" Actually, I had been wanting to visit this new place we'd moved close to, and Les wasn't one for window shopping, so I decided it would be nice to explore.

I wandered the streets of the Western city called Billings, passing antique shops and dress shops. I found a little pottery shop and went in. Inside, I found a wonderful clay teapot that had been glazed a brilliant red. I immediately decided to paint my kitchen yellow and add red accessories. I also purchased a set of red coffee mugs, some red plates, and even a red salt and pepper set. The little lady who had thrown the pottery herself was ecstatic. Her wares weren't cheap. She offered to pack them in tissue and bubble wrap and find boxes for me to transport them when Les could bring the Suburban by the shop later in the afternoon. They would be too heavy to carry around, so I agreed. I took my receipt and went across the street to a department store. In the linen department, I found a gingham tablecloth with a matching runner and then chose red-print placemats and napkins.

There was something powerful in shopping, but shopping and mania were wicked sisters. My blood was humming, and I knew I could go overboard if I wasn't careful. I tried to keep myself in check.

A few weeks before, I'd gone to Red Lodge to find Western items for my Western farmhouse.

I'd come home with plenty of typical kitschy stuff. The kinds of things all non-Montana people bought to put in their homes to make them look Montanan. The local retailers loved and hated us all at once. Les hadn't said much about the bill I'd presented to him when I was done. He probably figured he'd need to sell another painting or two.

In the department store across from the pottery shop, I found an awful crystal vase in the china department that looked just like it belonged in my mother's fashionable dining room. I bought it and had it sent to her. The trick to buying my mother gifts was deciding if I thought they were hideous. I could imagine, with delight, her exclamation that I'd actually found something she'd like in this god-forsaken-backwoods place we'd moved to.

After that, I found some silver bangle bracelets at the jewelry counter. They were mine now, after a quick zip-zip of the credit card. In the children's department, I bought Tamra Blue some flowered long johns. We didn't see those in Boston! I liked them so much I bought her a set in every color. Then I found some Superman tee-shirts for Adam. He got one of each design. For Les, I bought Levi's and snap-button shirts, the Western kind with the pearly buttons. I found him some leather gloves and wool socks. The clerks were just about drunk with glee as they flashed the credit card through the machine again and again. It was a quiet weekday in their lives, so I had plenty of help with my selections.

Sales. There were sales in the women's department. Amazing sales. Just ask my dazzled mind as I grabbed one sweater or shirt after the other in my size.

Finally, I looked up at the clock. My god, I was late meeting Les. I asked the more than accommodating sales woman to ring up my sale and wrap it so I could come back with Les and pick it up. She was happy to do so.

As I passed another sales counter, I saw a young mother with a baby and a toddler waiting. The clerk had been one of those that had helped me earlier. She had been lovely and smiling and very helpful. But as I passed, I saw a look of consternation on her face. I also noticed the look of defeat and embarrassment on the face of the young mother. In fact, on further investigation, her face was red and she looked about to cry. The tone of the clerk's voice was acid. "Well, you'll just have to talk to the manager, ma'am. Your account's been closed and there's nothing I can do about it! Now if you'll excuse me, I need to put all this merchandise back!" I glanced at the items the young woman had on the counter: children's clothes, a snowsuit, some cloth diapers. I didn't even know you could still get cloth diapers. I noticed the red sale tag on many of the items. I looked at the face of that clerk. She had been so sweet and gracious with me. She'd appreciated my suede jacket and my leather boots, my polished nails and neat hair. I'd never seen such a dejected look on anybody's face as I saw on that little mother, whose baby was starting to cry.

Without thinking twice, I handed the clerk one of my zillion credit cards. The young mom gasped as I said, "I cannot believe you are talking to this young woman in that tone of voice. How dare you! Take my card and wrap her purchase up immediately!" I hissed in my old courtroom voice. "And if I ever, ever hear you speak to another customer like that, I'll be speaking to your manager. In fact, where is your manager? I want to speak to your manager immediately!" The pitch of my voice was getting higher, louder. The toddler hid behind the mother and even she was stepping back.

In a moment, a young man in a dark suit appeared with wide eyes around the corner of a rack of clothes, a security guard with a silver badge behind him. I was still shouting at the now bawling clerk with all my venom. "Who the *hell* do you think you are?"

"What is the pr-problem, ma'am?" stuttered the man in the suit.

"It's your store clerk. She was very nice to me when I checked out because my card went through your little zippy machine. But when this woman had problems, she was vulgar and snapped at her. What? Are your clerks only paid to be human to the credit worthy?" The suited man glanced at the clerk and back at me. The woman with the children was still standing there. She was trying to shush her frightened children and calm herself. Her face was bright red.

I grabbed the receipt for her purchases and signed it. She found her voice and stammered, "No, ma'am. Really, it's okay. I'm sure it's all a misunderstanding. You needn't ..."

"Pack up her things and have someone bring them out to the car, and bring mine too," I snapped at the surprised security guard. "I should return every penny of everything I've bought today." I dropped a few of my packages as I reached for the hand of the little boy. "C'mon, honey, I'll take you and your mommy to your car." I began to march with him toward the door as his still-stunned mother followed me numbly. We got out into the air. I was shaking. The mother had tears streaking down her face. Behind us followed two sales boys with our packages, the man in the suit and the security guard.

"Where's your car, sweetie?" I said in a quieter tone to the mother. She abstractedly pointed to one just off the curb by the near parking meter. It was a beat up Ford Bronco with Wyoming plates. Inside, the upholstery had been taped together many times. "Well!" I snarled to one of the peach-faced store boys. "Put her packages in there!"

The suited man decided to speak. He told me he was sure it had all been a misunderstanding. I fumed at him with all my might.

"Your clerk was rude to this woman! There was no denying that. She was sweet as sugar to me, but she was nastier than shit toward this woman. I did not misunderstand!" He took a breath and began to apologize to me. I pointed toward the woman and the children. "Tell them." I said.

A second later, Les pulled up in our Suburban. He noticed the little group we made. The mother and the kids, the two store boys, the man in the suit, and the man with the badge … and me, his wife. First, Les looked startled, then he seemed to get a look of tired recognition on his face.

I ordered the boys to put my packages in the Suburban and I got in. The store manager was speaking to the woman as we drove off. I told Les to go to the ceramics store for the stoneware.

"What was that all about?" Les asked. But he sounded as if he wasn't sure he wanted to know.

I began to cry. I'd done it again. I told him the story. He just drove home. When we got to our house, he turned to look at me. He gathered me into his arms. After a bit, he said, "Show me what you bought today. Is it for the house? Let's go in and see."

That night, I dreamt about the incident in Boston.

My failure. The ultimate …

I wondered what I would have used if I hadn't grabbed Adam's baseball bat from the back seat of the car. Would I have used my foot, my hand … my briefcase? Would I have accomplished it?

I felt the bat as it hit the headlight.

That truly wonderful feeling as the wood hit the glass.

Then the delight, the absolutely sublime delight as I felt the tight wood make contact with the hood of that BMW.

I'd never known that windshields could shatter in such a melee of patterns before I beat the window in.

The pleasure … the pure pleasure of smashing in the top of the car.

The sirens.

Screaming, wailing. Red and blue lights in a disco-style frenzy as I beat the car.

The hysteria I felt as the cops grabbed me and tackled me to the ground.

Pepper spray stung.

And pissed you off.

I didn't remember being handcuffed.

I didn't remember being put into the back of the car.

I knew I ended up with quite a bump on my head. It was sore for days. Something told me I hit it on the doorframe of the cop car as I was pushed in.

In the jail cell—now that was a memory—I screamed with my face against the bars, swearing in language that was more forceful than the sewage spewing into a river.

Jumping and twisting, screaming and yelling until I was spitting blood.

Being rushed to the hospital after some impassable amount of time.

The straps tying me down.

The needle.

Waking up in straps.

I had peed myself while in the isolation ward in St. Elizabeth's psychiatric hospital.

"I couldn't save her."

It was so awful I couldn't look at Dr. Silverstein. I was in a stage of contrition by then. It's what happened after you went on a binge of high-flying anger.

I knew I'd screwed up.

The force of the mood swing left me all used up and sitting in the corner of a little room in a loony bin.

I didn't even know what possessed me to act so crazy.

Until they explained what they thought my symptoms were all about.

Post-traumatic Stress Disorder.

Manic symptoms.

That was me.

Extreme stress. It was a prisoner in the body that eventually fought its way out for escape.

Treatable, they assured me.

Work with the doctor, go to group meetings, start taking medication, attend the appointed court date to face down the judge whose BMW I smashed with my son's baseball bat.

Dr. Silverstein was kind. He had flawless white skin. He was rather delicate boned, with dark hair and clean, expressive hands. He emanated trust. I didn't have any choice anyway. If I didn't choose to stay in there, the judge could have me sent to jail. At least in this place I got to wear a little white gown that said St. Elizabeth Hospital on it and matching little gripper socks that said the same.

"Who couldn't you save?" Dr. Silverstein asked.

He had a nice voice. I began to cry. The whole scene passed before my mind. I was still pretty groggy with whatever the nurses had been using to sedate me. I told him the story of Melissa …

One day, Melissa walked into my office. She was well dressed and perfectly manicured. She was tiny. I asked her what I could do for her and she took off her large sunglasses. Somewhere in the hideous bruises of mottled brown, blue, and green, I saw desperate eyes. She could hardly talk. She put the glasses back on. I went around the edge of my desk and sat in the chair next to hers. I took her hand, all my professional decorum instantly swept away.

Knowing the answer, I still asked the question.

"Who did that to you, Melissa?"

The answer wasn't a surprise.

"Do you have children?" I asked next.

"Yes, one. A little girl, eighteen months old."

"Where is she now?" I asked.

"With the nanny. We are supposed to be at the park." Melissa spoke in a rushed voice.

"Is your daughter with the nanny at the park?" I wondered.

"Yes, the one down there." She pointed below my office to the general area of a little park that was located across the street from the office plaza.

"Does he know you're here?" was my next question.

"No, he went to New York for the day. My nanny set up this appointment. My name is not Melissa; it's her name. She set this up in her name ... you know, to protect me. Please don't let any of your staff know. If he finds out, he'll kill me."

She was deadly serious and shaking. She reached for a cigarette. Normally, I didn't allow smoking in my office, but at this moment, it was the least I could offer. I pulled over my coffee cup, which still had a little cold coffee in the bottom. I set it near the edge so she could use it for her ashes. She took in long, long drags and exhaled in huge billows of blue smoke.

"Melissa," I said as I watch the smoke swirl around her head like a guardian angel's shadow, "what do you want to do?"

She removed her glasses and looked right at me.

"My husband is Geoff Spencer. You've probably heard of him. His family owns half the commercial real estate in Boston. I don't have any money that's mine; it's all his. I don't have many choices here. For all I know, your firm is one that represents his corporation. But last night was it." She pulled back the bodice of her fine suite to show her bare skin. There were, of course, more achingly blue marks on her bosom. It was sickening.

I was silent for a moment, taking the situation in with her acrid cigarette smoke.

I was familiar with the Spencer Corporation, but knew right off that they weren't clients. Even though this was a situation that sounded like a bad movie, I already knew I'd take the case. It would be gut-wrenching and time consuming. I'd done lots of them. I often won, but not always. Sometimes it was the clients who gave in. They just gave up and went back. I never knew what happened after that. Well, not for sure. But it wasn't hard to guess.

"Do you have any family? Anywhere to go? Any way to support yourself?" I asked, but I knew the answers. Monsters like Geoff Spencer took over the lives of their women. Any power they may have had before the relationship began was slowly and meticulously, tortuously taken from them. Still, it was my duty to ask the same litany of questions. It was ethical to make the client understand that it might not work out as well as we all wanted it to.

She started to weep. I was scaring her to the point where she was ready to give up and leave. I explained I only want to be sure she knew what she is up against. It was bizarre to ask her this because she knew more about this than I ever would.

"We need to get your daughter in here and we need to call a shelter. Do you have any cash on you?" But, of course, the answer was no. Just a low-limit card, which was owned and tracked by the Spencer Corporation.

"I want you to walk over and get your daughter. Be very calm. I'll call a police escort for you if you like. If you don't want them involved, I understand. If you want to file charges, I will go with you to the station, and then we will get you to a shelter. You'll be safe. Once we get you settled there, we'll talk some more. But first, use the ATM in the lobby downstairs and cash out your card. They can't track where you spend cash. It's for you and your daughter's needs."

I could never tell if a woman in this predicament would walk out of my office and I would never see her again or if she'd go through with it. But "Melissa" seemed determined. She looked me in the eye and took one last drag of her cigarette. She exhaled and put it out in my cup.

"Please call the police," she said.

And the process began. But somehow, in the end, I was there in that hospital. Dried blood on my face and in my hair, in a locked room.

Serious charges being placed against me for assault against a judge, or rather his BMW.

Melissa and her child were dead.

"I couldn't save them," I said again to the doctor and wept uncontrollably.

In the morning, I rose from my bed. The old house, which was new to us, was chilly. I grabbed my chenille robe and padded downstairs to the kitchen, where Les was having his cigarette and drinking coffee. I sat foggily across from him.

"Rough night last night, Jo?" he asked between drags.

"Yes," I croaked out as I lifted a warm cup to my lips.

We heard a knock at the door. It was early for a visitor. The sun was barely peeking over the hills.

A blustery man came through the door. We recognized him as our neighbor to the north, Bob Conway. He stamped his heavy boots on the mat and Les welcomed him in with an offer of coffee.

"Don't mind if I do." He reminded me of Santa, with his graying beard and large mustache. He even had a wide girth. He sat down at the table and took note of Les's cigarette ashes, then he pulled out his pack and searched his pocket for his lighter.

His voice was loud. He would wake the kids, which was too bad because it was Saturday.

He inhaled and blew out smoke the color of his beard. "Say, you folks know you got a couple of fence posts down there near the creek close to my place?"

"You don't say." Les seemed surprised. He'd just been to the creek a couple of weeks ago.

"Yep," replied Conway. "Looks to me like maybe some stock have been working them fence posts 'til they're near lying on the ground." He took a loud sip of his coffee.

Montana men didn't drink their coffee with any particular delicacy, I'd noticed. That black-robed judge back in Boston was probably more refined.

Les lit another cigarette. Not usually allowed by me, but he knew I wouldn't object in front of a guest, so he took advantage.

"Well, ya' don't say. Guess I'd better go on up an' see. Noticed those posts were mighty ancient when I first saw that fence; figgered I'd be replacin' 'em come spring, before I turned the stock up there. Ya got any animules in that pasture?"

Conway was noisily drinking and smoking fast.

"Naw. Keep 'em closer to the barns this time of year, y'know. If'n yer in need of help repairin', jes let me know when you're ready. I got some twine and duct tape; we'll get it fixed right up." Conway winked and chuckled before taking another noisy slurp and another lusty inhale of his disappearing cigarette.

He then turned to look at me, still sitting there in my robe, my braid down the front of my shoulder. I must have been a sight. My mother would have had a fit to see me sitting there in my nighty at 7:00 a.m. with two cowboys, one of which I barely knew. It tickled me to think of it.

"I see ya got a mare out there ready to foal," he commented. Les had told him when we moved there that I had an interest in raising good horses for sale.

"Yes, Mr. Conway, my mare. She should be, around the first of the year. I've got two others that are near ready also." I smiled when I thought of my horses, especially Ashleigh's Grace.

"I know a fella outside Billings that could be in the market. I'll give him your name, long as you don't mind."

I didn't mind. I thanked him for it. Then I gently pushed my chair back and excused myself. The smoke and the loud slurping were a little too much for a Bostonian like me. Maybe I was a little like my mother.

As soon as I fed the kids breakfast, I decided to go for a ride. I'd have to take one of the geldings because I felt Ashleigh should rest. Adam asked if he could go with me. I decided I'd love his company and invited Tamra Blue also, but she didn't seem to have an interest. She asked Les if she could go with him and help oil some leather. I thought that was probably how it was always going to be. Me and Adam with our horses, Les and Tamra Blue with their art.

The cool air enfolded us as we settled into our saddles. Ashleigh whinnied after us with a hurt impatience at what she saw as abandonment. I had tried to explain to her that it wouldn't be long and we could go riding again.

Adam had my features. They were outlined against the bright blue Montana sky. The long nose, the green eyes, and the black hair. He would be handsome someday. At nine, he was about to get long and lanky. We talked a little. I suggested we go to the north fence and take a look at the damage.

The geldings were spirited. It was good that Adam was as secure a rider as I was. We broke onto the field, with its light, virgin snow cover. It would have been blinding but for our dark glasses and leather cowboy hats sitting low on our heads. I could smell the horses and leather from our jackets mingling with the pine trees and creek water. The air had those sparkly ice diamonds floating in it, like tiny little fairies.

Adam and I rode in companionable silence.

Adam. My son. I knew he trusted me more than Tamra Blue did. My craziness scared her, poor little thing. Adam accepted me. It didn't matter. When you're like me, you understand many of the boundaries other people feel because you wonder about them yourself. Tamra Blue was honest. She couldn't help that her mom was a nutcase sometimes. Still, I tried to be close to her, determined not to have the same mixed bag of animosity and love grow between her and me as was between my mother and me. But with Adam there was no barrier. He just liked to be with me. So we rode across the wide meadow, spotting mule deer and little rabbits, the occasional squirrel and mourning dove or pheasant. I loved it there.

I noticed she was running along beside us in the trees that lined the property. I wondered if I should say something to Adam. He didn't seem to recognize her presence, so I was silent.

We came upon the broken posts. We hopped off our horses and went for a closer look. The wood the posts were made out of was very old. Adam joked it might have been put up by cave men. As we took hold of one, we decided it was still sturdy enough to stand if we were to prop it with some rocks from a nearby rock pile. It would hold until we were able to fix the fence permanently. We pushed the post back into place.

"I'll hold it while you pile a few rocks," I told Adam.

He turned around and picked up a large stone. Just as he chose one, a flock of pheasants began to make loud, startling noises as if he had stepped in the middle of their shelter. He jumped and so did I. We took note of the hens scattering and squawking as they flew up into the cold air, out of their wintry home of bushes.

Just then, I saw her. Her eyes were ablaze. I'd never seen her like this. She looked almost excited, pleased even. Her thin body was tall and her sunken cheeks seemed to nearly fill out. It was eerie. The horses snorted and shuffled.

Adam shrugged and brought the stone over to the post. He laid it on the ground next to the bottom. I was still mesmerized by the sight only I seemed to notice in the bushes behind him. He kept picking up stones and stacking them. Each time he did, she would become even more agitated and excited.

"Mom!" It was Adam. He stood stock-still. He was pointing at the ground and his face was stricken pale.

Later, after we had called the sheriff, I hugged Adam. I didn't think they would have believed me if he hadn't been there. With what we'd seen, I was sure even Les would have wondered if I was imagining something.

Adam had dropped to his knees. At first I didn't see it. He moved a rock aside, and there it was, the bones of fingers on a skeletal hand gently lying on a mound of dirt as if caressing it. Adam and I looked at it in amazement and fright, and then searched each other's faces. I moved a few more rocks and saw more bone, a wrist, all the way up to an elbow. I stopped there and looked around, but she wasn't there. I heard the squawk of one of the pheasants in the adjoining pasture. Then I sat down on the ground, the snow soaking through my Levied bottom.

"What should we do, Mom?" Adam asked, still staring at the exposed bones. "Who do you think it is?" he asked, incredulous, without taking his eyes off the sight.

I had my idea suddenly but couldn't say it.

"We'd better cover her ... I mean ... it," I said. "We shouldn't disturb it more."

Gently, I patted a small mound of dirt and snow over it and placed a bandanna on top of it with rocks to hold the edges of the bandanna in place. I didn't put the rocks on top of the bone.

Adam and I rode back to the house and told Les about what we had found.

When the sheriff drove up, Les and Adam went out to the porch to meet him. I stood at the screen and listened. Tamra Blue was wide-eyed as she listened to Adam tell what had happened.

"Mama, it's your ghost," she said.

"What?" I looked into those blue-blue eyes.

"It's the one I heard you tell Daddy about. It's her."

The sheriff heard part of her comment and turned to look at us.

I shushed her. No sense in everyone in this community knowing I was a nutso.

The sheriff went back to talking to Adam and then he asked me a few questions.

"Did I hear you say you might know something about the bones?"

"No," I said sheepishly. "Just a silly story I told my kids ... you know, ghosts and stuff, Halloween." My comment rather trailed off.

The sheriff asked us to take him to the scene.

We all got in his Blazer and drove toward the north fence line.

Once there, Adam and I walked gingerly to the little mound of rocks. We showed the sheriff the post we'd been working on, and Adam was explaining how he'd been getting the rocks from where we'd seen the bones.

It was then that I saw her, sitting in the tree branches where the pheasants roosted. She was staring at me with her empty eyes.

The sheriff was speaking into his shoulder, where he had his little radio secured. He spoke in code about having a finding at the Porter ranch. "Do you copy me?" he ended.

A static reply came: "Copy. Do you need assistance? Over?"

"Yes, let's get a deputy and contact Will Taylor at the coroner's. Over."

"Copy. I'll get an officer out. Over."

"Copy and out."

Sheriff Lind was a short huff of a man, with brownish skin, a fat nose, a little fuzzy caterpillar mustache, and silvered black, wavy hair. He had dark eyes and wasn't wearing a hat.

He scratched at his thickly haired scalp.

"Well, folks, by the looks of it, it's not in bad shape, which probably means it may not be very old. It's hard to say. I've asked the dispatcher to notify the coroner. We'll go from there."

He began to walk back to the Blazer. Adam's and Tamra Blue's eyes were glued to the still-visible skeletal arm. Tamra looked frightened. I held her head to my breast. As I looked up, she was still in the tree. She saw me hugging Tamra Blue, and I could have sworn I saw a look of longing on her face.

Who knows what intuition is in us sometimes? Especially in women, mothers. It was a natural movement that I made; I motioned with my gloved hand for her to come to me. She did. Like a shy little puppy, she gingerly made her way out of the tree and over the little creek. She stepped over the mount of rocks and stood very close. It was like she was hovering just outside my skin. She was achingly cold, but I didn't flinch. I was afraid if I did she would go away. And right at that moment, I knew she needed me not to flinch but to stand strong and warm.

We got back into the Blazer and the sheriff took us back to the house. I held her presence close as if it were delicate glass. I also made sure Tamra Blue was snuggled into my other side. Les was watching me. Adam sat up front with Sheriff Lind and asked a million questions about all the gizmos on the dash.

Tamra Blue was clearly upset. I soothed her and told her it would be alright. Nothing to be frightened of. Nothing.

Once in the house, I took my coat off carefully. I couldn't see her, but I knew she was there.

"Come sit in the kitchen," I said to her. The kids thought I was talking to them. I made lunch.

All that day, she watched me. She lingered in

the corners behind the furniture or with her legs stuck up underneath her gown as she stayed near the ceiling.

Tamra Blue was clinging and unsettled the whole day. I finally calmed her to sleep that night.

The sheriff and his entourage had been back and forth all afternoon. Finally, in the twilight, he made his way to the porch and spoke to Les. They lit cigarettes and talked for about fifteen minutes. The little lit ends glowed in the late blue light, like little lasers.

Les came in and shook off his coat. He took off his boots. I was at the kitchen sink rinsing mugs. He walked up behind me and kissed my neck. He wrapped his arms around me. His breath still smelt of tobacco.

"Well, I didn't get much done today," he said with his head on my shoulder. We both chuckled.

"What about the sheriff; what did he find out? Did he say?"

"Wouldn't say much. Just that they would be back tomorrow to see if they could get the remains. The ground is pretty frozen. They need to get a special contraption to thaw out the ground."

"Do they know who it is?" I asked.

"Don't know. He wouldn't say much. Y'know they don't want a bunch of people up there or want us to mess with it. There's a deputy on watch tonight. That's about all he said."

"Hmmmm," was my pensive reply.

I turned in his arms and put my arms around him.

"Are you feeling something about this, Jo?" he said quietly.

I could only seem to hang my head and shrug my shoulders.

"It's just that ... well ... you and your ... dreams and stuff. Then today ... I swear you were watching something, and when you were hugging Tamra Blue by the fence ..." I looked into his eyes. It was hard to be married to someone who had wild dreams and thoughts.

"I'm not sure what I think, Les," was all I could say. It was true.

We kissed.

"It's time to get some sleep," he said, stroking my hair.

I loved this man and his beautiful eyes, the way he looked at me from down deep, the way his hair fringed his collar, the way he always smelled of tobacco and leather, the curly hair on his chest through the vee of his open shirt. I rested my forehead there and let my thoughts dissolve into his heart.

The moon was white and beautiful. There were no clouds in the sky. Just twinkly pinpricks of stars. I wasn't used to such night skies. At our ranch just outside of Red Lodge, Montana, the stars were very close. As if I could reach up and grab one.

I sat in the dining room staring out at the

naked moon as it bathed in its sea of stars. I envied it its solidness. It really existed. We knew it did because astronauts had actually walked on it and brought back rocks. We had not just imagined it

I knew I would not sleep tonight. I had checked on Tamra Blue and Adam. Les had fallen asleep as soon as we were done making love.

So it was just me, the moon, and the girl who was pacing across the yard.

"Who are you?" I whispered.

Through the glass, she seemed to hear me. She stood quietly and stared at me. I went to the window and pressed my face and hands up against it.

"Come and talk to me," I said. "Please. I want to know."

Ghosts were funny. They couldn't really talk. But they could tell you things.

She began to pace back and forth some more, faster and faster. She seemed so frightened.

That ghost.

I decided to put my coat on and go outside. I stuck my bare feet into my snow boots and went out on the porch.

She was still pacing by the fence that enclosed our yard.

I approached her. She didn't run. We came to stand about three feet from each other.

"Look," I said quietly, "I want to know what is keeping you here. Why do you let me see you?"

Her face began to contort. I grabbed the fence for support. I remembered Melissa's face the last time I saw her alive. The confusion and questions in her eyes.

Suddenly, she began to sob. I wanted to reach out to her, but my hands were terrified and clinging to the wood on the board fence.

For only a moment, one awful, slicing stinging moment, she turned to me. There was red blood running out of her forehead and onto her gown. It soaked into her white body from the rivulets formed as it ran down her neck, between her breasts, and over her round belly. She was more than horrifying. We both began to scream. We screamed and screamed into that that terrible night. Our voices flying upwards and snapping in the icy air.

Les caught me as I began to crumple to the ground.

"Josephine! For shit's sake! Stop this; stop this now. You're just too … fucked for words. Stop it!" Somehow, his voice found me. I looked around, but she was gone. I clung to Les. The leather of his jacket soaked by my tears and saliva.

"C'mon now. For Chrissake, you scared the shit outta me this time, woman! Out here screaming like a …"

"Like a what, Les?" I screamed back. "Like a crazy bitch?"

We were both shaking.

"Have you been takin' that medication?" He was so scared his face was as pale as the moon. He was angry too.

He sunk to his knees and began to cry. I wanted to slap him.

"Yes, I've been taking the meds. But this is more than that. If I wasn't already crazy, I could make you believe. But that person up on the north fence ... it's her. Something happened to her; I saw her. It isn't right. I just feel it. She is ... well, she's ... been hurt or something."

"*Jesus*, Josephine! This is nuts. There is no such thing as ..."

"As what, Les?" I sobbed. "As ghosts?"

"Yeah," he said. "Jo, I love you. But you're not right. Ever since that thing happened back in Boston. I think you need more help."

"Well, fine, Les. You think I'm crazy. Just say it. You do! Well, honey ... I got news for you. I fucking know I'm crazy. But what about her?"

"Her who?" he asked exasperated. "Melissa? Or whatever her name was?"

"No, not Melissa, Les. Her!" I motioned with my hands in the air around me. "The one I see. The one who is buried up there. She was bleeding from her forehead."

He stood shakily. He put his hands on his thighs and kept his head low. He was shaking with sobs and cold. He turned toward the barns and said, "I'm going to check on the horses. Get back to the house."

I sat at the kitchen table wrapped in my coat, my feet back in my slippers. I sat that way all the rest of the night. Les didn't come back in. I knew he'd gone out to his shop for a bottle and to be away from me, his crazy wife.

The sun rose in brilliance. It covered the landscape with its daytime freshness. It made the night seem impossible.

I put out some cold cereal and bowls for the kids. I went upstairs and crawled into the shower.

Later that day, the sheriff was back on the porch. I hadn't spoken to Les all day. I presumed he was still in the shop.

"Well, Mrs. Porter, we exhumed the body." His voice was heavy on the "u." He dragged it out like it was a long vowel. I could almost see the little long vowel mark from my phonics class in grade school hang over his head.

"Do you know who it is?" I asked.

"I'm not allowed to give details at this point, ma'am," he said politely.

"Sheriff Lind, would you and your deputy like a fresh cup of coffee and a slice of cake. Seems like you've had yourselves a day."

He looked at his watch. "Mrs. Porter, that would be wonderful."

"Then tell the other officer to come on in," I said.

I understood he couldn't give information about what his crew was working on or what they might know. But I decided I would try to get a good start at some clue. I would use a few gentle tactics I'd learned practicing law. Maybe she couldn't tell me, but this sheriff might.

We sat at the table and I served the cake and coffee. Les had decided to come around. He greeted the officers and poured himself a cup of coffee before he sat down, not looking at me once. He looked rough. He must've drunk the whole bottle, I thought. It was nearly four in the afternoon. The late afternoon sun was mild and getting weak.

I started interrogating carefully. The sheriff and his deputy were cautious but willing to talk a little.

"Are you familiar with any of the former owners of this ranch?" I asked. They were. They could describe what they knew of the original homesteaders, who still had family in the area, on down to the owners just previous to us.

"A few years ago, a man by the name of Kent Platt bought this place and decided to try his luck ranching. The place was pretty run-down about then, so he got it fairly cheap. Not that anything is cheap. He and his wife or girlfriend put some work into fixing it up. Eventually, the woman moved out, and he eventually put up the For Sale sign and left."

Despite my best attempt at casually cajoling information out of them, they were tight-lipped and resistant to most questions, except when I asked if they'd like more cake, which they accepted. The only other question I asked was where they were taking the remains. "To the state crime lab. They should pretty much be able to tell us everything we want to know."

I refilled the coffee cups and passed the sugar and cream.

"How can we help?" I asked.

"Well, the area by your fence has been swept for evidence. But we still don't want folks up there. Once the story gets in the news, you're bound to have some Lookie Lous snooping around, so I'd suggest a lock on your gate. We'll be asking for leads or information, so if anyone stops and asks you for details or has questions, just refer them to us. "

Both Les and I nodded our agreements. And then I asked, "The woman you mentioned having lived here, where did she go? And what happened to Mr. Platt?"

"Well, we're going to have t'do some checkin' t'see if he's around, and the same with her. We'll let you know how things progress. And I'm sure they will progress. That skeleton's in pretty good shape to be very old."

He gulped the remainder of his coffee and declined my offer for more cake, and both officers rose to leave.

My emotions and intuitions were alive like electricity sizzling in a rainstorm.

She was aware too. She sat on a tree branch in our yard and watched as the men drove down the lane and turned onto the highway and were gone. She stayed in that tree until nighttime. Then I didn't know where she went. It was quite some time before I saw her again.

I spent the next few days in the barn. It was

time to start paying attention to my end of the ranch business that Les and I had invested in. I felt stronger and better every day. I spent Monday afternoons in Lola's office, but other than that, I was busy with the horses. Our phone was unlisted. It was a good thing.

The local papers buzzed with the story of how Adam and I had found a corpse on our property. A search for Kent Platt was underway. He'd left the area not too long after his woman had left. There was also a search for her. Sometimes news reporters came to the house to ask questions. I was experienced with handling them from my former practice. It was easy for me to be pleasant when I said, "No comment," or, "We don't know anything the paper hasn't already printed."

Though I had cautioned Adam to be careful with who he gave information to, he did enjoy becoming sort of a hero at school. He liked to mesmerize the kids with the story of how he and his mom had been fixing a fence when he'd noticed the skeletal hand. Finally, Les and I were called to the school because some of the kids had been scared by the story and their parents had complained. We'd had to shut his storytelling down quickly. Also, Tamra Blue was frightened. She had a hard time sleeping. Many nights I lay down with her until she was soundly asleep. Sometimes we would read an extra story or talk. We spent time together that would not have otherwise been found if not for the whole incident. For the first time, I felt like Tamra Blue began to settle down and wanted to be close to me. It was just easier for a kid to have a parent who was not bashing in car windows with bats.

The holidays passed without incident and I kept myself constantly busy. I worked the horses and cleaned the stalls. I babied and cared for my pregnant mare like she was a goddess. I thought about the woman who was said to have left Kent Platt. I made inquiries of our neighbors and searched for information. Bob Conway's wife remembered her. The information she shared with the sheriff's detective she also shared with me. What she told me sent shivers down my spine.

Georgette Conway remembered the young woman who was with Platt when they moved to the ranch. She said her name was Emily and that she had been pregnant the last time Georgette had seen her. Georgette commented that she seemed to be in her twenties and was rather quiet and kept to herself. She also mentioned that Kent Platt had been known to be a drinker and that he'd spent more than a night or two in jail. Not long after Emily left, Platt sold the ranch.

The time that I'd seen her with the blood running from her head, I had noticed a round belly underneath the floaty, white dress I always saw her in.

One sun-bright afternoon, I noticed Ashleigh's Grace was getting close when I went out to do the chores. As soon as I fed the kids some quick macaroni and cheese for dinner, I returned to the stable to be with her. I told the kids to do the dishes and their homework and to come on out if they wanted to.

It wasn't a hard birth. It was her first, though, and she was a little nervous. I could sense it when I talked to her and touched her. I'd had time to read up on foaling and knew what to do for the most part. I had also interviewed some veterinarians around the area to find one I could work with on a permanent basis. It was actually Lola who put me in contact with the one I chose. It was a relative of hers who specialized in prized stock. The vet and I had visited on the phone about Ashleigh as I was making dinner that day. She went through the steps of what to watch for and gave me her number so I could reach her if I had questions.

At one point, Ashleigh looked into my eyes as we waited. I knew she was glad I was there. Her confidence in me gave me confidence in myself. Confidence was something I realized I'd been missing for many months, ever since the judge had told me I should consider disbarment over jail time or probation. I stroked her fine head and crooned to her, careful to respect her need to not be disturbed or over-intruded upon.

I thought of Melissa and her daughter.

I thought about the skeletal remains we'd found in the pasture.

I thought of the pain and heartache I had caused Les and the kids with my crazy behavior.

I thought of Tamra Blue and Adam. I even thought of my mother. What of the endless rift between her and me? I barely remembered my father, he'd left us when I was small. I blamed my mother. Perhaps she blamed me.

But mostly, I just felt the warm, brown light of the stable and kept track of the breaths and shudders of my beautiful Ashleigh.

After a time, Adam and Tamra Blue crept quietly to the gate. Ashleigh was getting close and snorted at their presence. She was alert and taut. The kids stayed back and kept silent.

A short while passed and Ashleigh began to labor harder. It was time. I crept softly to her hindquarter and felt up to where the little colt's head was beginning to crown. Ashleigh began to grunt and whinny. It was a strange and frightening sound. True pain. I was hard at my work when, out of the corner of my eye, I saw her on the rafter above me, watching what was going on. She was focused on the horse. Silently, she slid down to be nearer. I acknowledged her presence, and she stepped closer to Ashleigh, who seemed to sense her presence also.

Ashleigh began to push herself up halfway on her shanks, wheezing and panting. Then she lay down again as the woman's airy hands reached to guide her and began stroking her face the way I had done. Ashleigh seemed to calm in her presence. She buried her face in Ashleigh's neck. Within moments, the head of the colt began to appear. It was glossy and wet as it broke through a cloud of mucus. With a few giant gusts of air from Ashleigh, it was pushed entirely out. New colts always looked sort of disappointing at first. They looked like thin little twigs all covered in slime. Ashleigh caught her breath a moment and then turned to observe her young one. I remained a respectful distance away.

Tamra Blue's and Adam's heads were propped up at the top of the wooden gate as they observed with wide eyes. We all watched silently for several minutes. Even the ghost woman. She had climbed back on the rafter, one leg hanging down and her arms outstretched to grasp the ceiling. She looked like an angel. She watched with a glowing tenderness in her eyes. I wondered about the baby they said Kent Platt's wife had been expecting.

Now Ashleigh was trying to help the colt stand. It was always a little pitiful to watch a colt's struggle with this. But eventually they always stood, coughed, stumbled, and then, hopefully, nursed. The little foal did all of these things.

The air was heavy with the smell of horse sweat and blood. Little stickers of hay clung to both mother and baby. I looked up in the rafters and noticed she was crying. Soft droplets rose out of her eyes and fell like raindrops on Ashleigh's colt. I was hoping she wouldn't start lamenting too loudly and scare the horse or children the way she'd done me. She didn't. She just stayed where she was and wept.

I quietly told the children to go back to the house to bed, which they did with reluctance, but I stayed another hour or so. Ashleigh seemed comfortable in her new role as a mother and things seemed normal. I cleaned up the stall a little, not wanting to disturb the mother and baby. Then I gathered my things and shut the stall gate softly,

"Good job, Ashleigh. You did a good job," I said.

She whinnied low and inclined her head to me. I gently patted her snout and looked toward the ceiling, but it was empty.

I washed up in the stable sink after I put my rubber gloves and clean rags away. I threw out the bloodied ones. The water in the barns was extra hot. I walked out into the night air and looked around. Les was still in his shop working. He'd been out early on to check on Ashleigh and me. He was in the middle of a large order of saddles. I went to tell him the news.

Once inside the warmth of the workshop, I breathed in the scent of leather, oils, and paints. They were the smells that came in with Les every evening. He looked up from his project, a beautiful riding saddle for someone back east. Its intricate designs were amazing. He looked like a dark god as he peered over its edge, his black eyes focusing on me. I smiled.

He walked toward me. I noticed he had lost some weight. His belt buckle didn't seem to be cutting into his belly as much.

"I don't have to ask." He grinned. "I can tell

from those big, shiny eyes that everything went well." He reached for me.

"It went very well," I said, welcoming his arms around me. I was exhausted and elated.

He kissed me soundly on the lips. Then he stood back and looked at me.

"Woman, you've got blood 'n' shit all over you!" We both laughed. "What say we go wash all that stuff off of you and put you to bed." He grabbed a bottle of whiskey from the shelf and took a big swig.

"Here's to my wife, the horse doctor and ghost tamer!" he said as he handed me the bottle. I couldn't help but giggle at his remark.

I didn't really like strong drink but did take a good-sized swallow of it. It made me shiver as it drained down the back of my throat. He took another swig and I did too.

"That's enough of that!" I said as I flinched the second drink down. "If I didn't know better, I'd say you were trying to get me drunk," I flirted.

"Smart for a lawyer," he said as he put his tools away.

"Ex-lawyer," I remarked.

"Well, at any rate, it's time you and I had a little middle of the night time together, starting with that bath!"

We walked back to the house with our arms around each other. I felt giddy from the whiskey and the events in the horse stable. It was wonderful to have Les's arm around me and his warm liquor and tobacco breath in my hair.

A few days later, the sheriff came by. I acknowledged him from the stable doors and invited him in. I showed him into the stall where Ashleigh stood proudly nursing her sturdy foal. The sheriff admired both animals.

"It's a girl!" I exclaimed with pride. He smiled at me. We were nearly the same height. I was covered with dust and straw; my boots were caked with worse. He seemed as used to it all as I was, so we continued to talk about the horses until finally I pushed past him a little and put my shovels and pitchforks away. It occurred to me that he was watching my backside as I did this. I turned sharply to catch him doing it. He immediately cleared his throat and sort of guffawed in embarrassment. I picked up the barn phone and dialed Les's extension in the workshop.

"Les, Sheriff Lind is here," I announced.

We gathered around the kitchen table after I'd removed by boots and washed my hands. Les was pouring coffee.

"What can you tell us?" I asked as I sat down for the first time all day.

"Well, I can talk about what's public," he said as he took a long sip from his mug.

I waited without asking more questions. I put my chin on my hand and studied him. He leaned back a bit in his chair.

"The former owner, Platt, is wanted for

questioning. As you know, he owned the place about the same time that the remains date back to. The woman he'd been with, when he said she'd left him, there wasn't any reason to question that she'd left or where she went. You know, when no one comes lookin' for someone, there ain't a reason to question anything. And no one ever made any missing person's report on a woman named Emily Platt. If she had another last name, no one seems to know it." He shook his head.

"You think it might be her?" Les asked.

"Can't say for sure. Mostly, we're speculatin'," the sheriff replied. "We'd like to talk to her if we can find her. We may have to begin a media search for her or anyone who knows her. "

"How did this person found in our pasture die?" I asked, knowing he may not tell me. But he did.

"A young female, early twenties. She was about eight or nine months pregnant. Shot to the top of her head at close range. I think we are looking at two deaths …" He trailed off shaking his head.

I heaved a large sigh, almost a sob.

Suddenly, Les's eyes were focused full on me. Like flies stuck on flypaper.

The sheriff didn't notice; he looked genuinely sorry. Country folks weren't as opaque about their feelings as someone from the East Coast might have been, I thought.

"What about Platt?" I asked.

"Well, we think he might be somewhere in

the Northwest using another name. We haven't tracked him down."

"Which means you suspect him of foul play," I stated.

"We just want to talk to him for now. But I will say the angle of the wound—well, there's no way a person can do that themselves."

"Not to mention how they were buried," Les commented.

"What will happen next?" I asked.

"Well, the word is out for Platt. That's our main interest at this time. We're also looking for the woman named Emily. The FBI is involved at this point and it's theirs now. So we wait for information as it comes."

"What should Les and I be doing?"

"Just what you've been doing. Keep your eyes and ears open. You never know what will come up."

Later, as I lay in bed next to Les, my heart filled with unspeakable dread. I fell asleep after hours of staring at the ceiling.

I was pulled into a dark place, a swirling world of women and children all reaching toward me and crying. I went around and around looking at all their blurred faces, trying to make out their features. Who were they? At one point, I saw Melissa and her daughter. "Rena!" I called. It was her real name. I reached out to them, but they were whisked away in the current. I couldn't save them.

Finally, I arrived at the center of the current. There was a woman there. She looked to be caressing her large abdomen. She was a beautiful woman, with fair skin and dark hair. She had a thin frame. Inside her a child grew. I could see it through her skin. It was meant to be a sweet child, with glossy curls and bright eyes. The mother looked up into my face, her eyes a beautiful blue ... Tamra Blue. I jumped back in terror. In a moment, a strange crack shattered through the space I was in. Then in the next second, the woman's head exploded. Bits of bone and tissue splattered across my face and chest. It was hideous to feel the warm flesh and blood make contact with my skin. I was spitting pieces of it out of my mouth when I saw the child. Inside its mother it was still alive. In the next moments, dirt was being flung over the body of the mother, but I could still see the child. It shimmered and rolled inside its mother. It struggled for its life. It strove to live. I watched as it literally withered away, like an un-watered plant.

Somewhere, my own screams filled my ears. I was fighting the current of faces and bodies.

And then Les woke me. I was covered in sweat. I was weeping uncontrollably and gasping to explain. I couldn't save them.

I didn't dare go back to sleep that night. I sat wrapped in a quilt on the couch and then I turned to see her in the corner of the room watching me.

"Emily," I whispered, "Emily, this must stop."

She didn't seem surprised that I knew her name now.

"You must let me know what I can do to help

you. Because this cannot go on. You deserve to be free. I deserve to be free. Please let me help you." I began to weep and so did she. She crept over and sat next to me. We sat very close together, though we could not feel each other's touch.

We sat like that a long time until I fell asleep.

On my next visit with Lola, I spoke about the investigation and my thoughts surrounding the events that had taken place. I told her about Emily's reaction to the birth of Ashleigh's foal. I told her about telling Emily that she needed to let me know how to help her. I told her about the dream I'd had.

Lola was very patient. That day, she asked me to consider something.

"I like that you asked this 'Emily' what you can do to help her. But there is something else that I want you to ask her." She waited for my response.

"What's that? Should I ask her if she could say hello to your dead relative or something?"

Lola laughed. "Jo, you are such a joker. No, what I want you to ask this spirit is, what can she do to help you?" I looked up in surprise.

"How would that even be possible?"

"Well, sometimes in the Native spirituality, when a spirit continues to wander the earth, it is because they are not free yet. You have told me that you have sensed that the spirit of Emily is not free. Perhaps if the spirit is allowed to help someone or do something positive, it may be allowed its passage. You should ask Emily to help you."

"What should I ask for help with?" I was serious. "I don't believe that she is part of a deity that could have power over my life, like Jesus or Mary. She is just a little wayward spirit who is lost."

"Jo," said Lola, "think about your dream. Think about the incident in the store with the clerk and the young mother; think about Melissa and her daughter; think about Emily and her baby; think about you and your children and even about your relationship with your mother."

I thought about the possible connections. Like connecting stars in the sky with a white streak pen. Lola continued.

"There are links here. You are mourning the loss of your client, Melissa, and take that loss as a personal failure. For some reason, you have not only connected with the spirit of another woman who was possibly murdered, but you may have actually helped her ... and she is dead!"

I considered the coincidence.

"You joke about your mother a lot, but in turn, you also worry about your relationship with your own daughter. Notice how all the parties are women and children. Jo, I think your own spirit has a natural potential to want to reach out and do something positive. The challenge is that you consider yourself crazy because of your diagnosis. Your license to practice law was taken from you because of your violent reaction to your belief that the system had basically killed Melissa and her daughter. But being a lawyer isn't all you are and having a mental health diagnosis doesn't mean you're crazy. There is so much more to you than these two things. I think your own spirit knows this and is speaking through Emily. I think you should take some time to think about ways in which to find healing for yourself through this situation. You might be surprised at the strength and insight you gain. Do you understand what I am saying?"

I nodded a little numbly.

She continued, "I do encourage you to really consider what I've said and think about what it means to give yourself permission to heal from the past and start over." The silver barrette in her inky black hair caught the edge of the late afternoon sun. It almost blinded me for a moment, *or* perhaps it was the tears that were starting to build behind my eyes.

I agreed that I would give it all some thought; though, I corrected one thing she said; I thought I should. "You know, Melissa, whose real name was Rena, committed suicide by inhalation of carbon monoxide fumes in her car with her baby girl in her lap. It was the same day the judge awarded custody to Geoff Spencer." I began to weep. Lola patted my hands.

"So who really killed her?" I blubbered. "Yes, she felt hopeless. The system failed her. I was part of that system and I failed her and her child. The judge failed when he said Geoff was allowed custody of the child. I still think he took a bribe. There was something not right. Of course, when

I learned of her death, I smashed his fucking car! My actions didn't make it right."

"Jo, I hate to tell you this, but you are not a savior. None of us are. It was not your job to 'save' her, but you did try to 'help' her." She was speaking close to my ear in a rich, soothing voice. "Did you do everything possible in your control to help Melissa get away from her abuser?"

"Yes," I bawled, "but she's still dead."

"Do you think you could have changed her decision, really?" she asked.

I thought about this a moment as my tears dropped to the carpeting as I held my head in my hands. The pain in my heart was unbearable.

Finally, I blew my nose.

"Other than actually being there when she decided to lock herself and her daughter in the car in the garage and take her and her child's life, what else could you have done?"

"I'd have gotten her out of there. I'd have taken her away. I would have given them money and helped them escape."

"Jo, listen to me." Lola lifted my face up to hers. Our noses were about three inches apart. "Didn't you do all those things? Think about it. You did all those things. You've told me so before. You gave her money for things she couldn't get at the shelter, you gave her rides to court, you got her divorce granted, and you cared about her. What else could you have done besides move in with her and guard her every moment? Chances are that wouldn't have worked either."

I blew my nose some more.

"Jo, you are an educated, sensitive, and intelligent woman. You need to give yourself credit for the things you did right. You, my dear woman, are a helper, but if you expect you're going to 'save' everyone, living or dead, from their sorrows, you will never heal. I know this may sound harsh, but you are also wrong if you think you have that much control over other people's situations. This assumption about yourself is very disempowering, and frankly, it's more about you than it is about your client, or your loved one, or your ghosts, for that matter." She began to pat my back as I grabbed another tissue.

"You must understand that some situations just go beyond our control. In fact, most situations do. We do what we can. I believe you did everything you could for your client Melissa. You are familiar with the amount of depression and trauma that are associated with domestic violence. Many women survive and many don't. Your Emily may be one of those who didn't survive. Not her fault and not yours either." I began to look Lola in the eyes, even though I was hiccupping by then.

"Jo, maybe you're being given a gift," Lola continued. "Emily, or whoever she is, didn't have you when she was physically alive, but now she has you when she still needs you. She needs you to tell her story. She needs your strength. For whatever reason, she exists in your heart and mind, or out there in your trees or your barn. She is there for a reason. Find out and go with it. It will be good for you. I'm sure of it."

That night, I began to sob again as I put my head onto Les's shoulder. He held me a long time without saying anything. I couldn't vocalize the pain I felt. As always, he was quietly understanding and didn't ask for an explanation.

A few days later, the authorities in some little town in Texas located Kent Platt. He was living under the name Ken Price. He had a wife and a young son. He was questioned about the disappearance of Emily. In the beginning, he had denied any knowledge of a person named Emily. But then authorities told him they knew of his time in Montana and his ownership of property and that he had been known to be in the company of a woman named Emily. They told him they needed to find her and asked for his knowledge of the baby and where they could get information from her family.

Kent Platt was caught. Emily Platt had died during one of his drunken fits. She was expecting a baby, and he had accused her of sleeping around. When she tried to deny it, he admitted that he had "shot the lying bitch." When he realized what he had done, he panicked and took her body to the north field and buried it. He figured she'd never be found and told the locals she'd left him.

The story made headlines everywhere. Someone from the Northwest who'd known Emily produced pictures of her. Others who'd known Emily were interviewed, and pictures of her shined back from a newspaper Les brought home from town one evening. But I already knew her. I knew what she looked like.

Her pretty smile and the brightness in her eyes were the only things foreign to me about the pictures. Everything else looked familiar, her dark brown hair, her tall, thin build. She had grown up in Spokane, Washington. She'd been shuffled around a lot between foster homes as a child. The only people who seemed to know much about her were some former coworkers at a guest ranch close to the Idaho border. They spoke about her love of horses and that it was how she had met Kent. He was a slick-looking rodeo cowboy who rode the circuits a lot. One of the coworkers told the detectives that Kent had seemed very nice, very courteous and sweet to Emily. After the two of them had moved in together, he told her it was time to quit her job. Then they had abruptly married and moved to some place in Montana, and the people with whom she'd been close to at the guest ranch never heard from her again. No one stepped forward as family to Emily.

Oh, Emily, I thought. *No wonder you are such a lost little soul.*

Kent Platt was charged with the murder of his wife and her baby.

No one claimed their remains. I made a request to be allowed to take charge of them. After much red tape, I was allowed to have them. I paid for their cremation.

Meanwhile, it was time to name the little foal that Ashleigh had given birth to just weeks before. She was a fine little thing, all black and shiny. On her haunches were splatters of white-paint spots. Not detectable at first; you had to look for them. I remembered seeing Emily's tears fall on her the night the foal was born.

Late one evening, I put a light jacket on and went into the watery green, spring evening as it began to drowse with the sunset. I walked out to the barn to check the horses, Ashleigh and her foal in particular. I saw Emily there too. She was standing next to the foal. The horses had no concern, even though they seemed to be sniffing at her presence. I propped myself against a post and looked at her. I began to talk to her as if she were my neighbor.

"They found him, Emily. They found Kent. We know what happened to you and your baby. I know your story now. My friend Lola advises me that I should ask for your help so you'll be free to go. I don't know what to ask for really. I guess I do want to know I've helped you and that you can be at peace … so that I can be at peace. What do you say, Emily? Can you do that for me?"

I couldn't tell if she heard me or if she understood. She was stroking the little colt's mane. It was the same color as her hair was in the photos.

After a time of me standing there watching her

and her seeming oblivious to my presence or my request, she moved toward me. I stood stock-still. Afraid and yet ...

A warm feeling passed through me. For a moment I stood in a dazzling white light that had this strange sort of gentleness in it. Strange because it was both very soft but very strong. I saw Melissa and her little girl waving at me from across time and space, their smiles glowing softly. Peace all around them. Emily flew up, spreading her arms to the night-blue sky, her soft image gently moving with the light breeze. Suddenly, I felt Emily break loose. I felt her freedom, her silent drifting away. And for the first time, I heard her voice, a soft delicate lullaby rustling through the trees, but only for an instant or two.

And then she was gone.

A few days later, I spread Emily's and her baby's ashes around my yard and the corrals. I wanted her near me always.

It was time to put Emily to rest and name the little filly. I decided to call her Emily's Peace and wrote it on the colt's registry card.

I asked Tamra Blue if she would like to keep the horse for her own. Her blue eyes lit up like the sky with sun in it. She asked if I would give her some more riding lessons.

And so it was that I gave the colt I'd named Emily's Peace to my daughter, Tamra Blue.

Silent Night

JULIET DROVE DOWN THE HIGHWAY ON THE COLD December night. The day had been spent in the city shopping with the kids. It had been a bitterly cold but clear blue day. The skift of snow reflected in jewel-like crystals from the first quarter moon. It was extraordinary that only a small slice of moon could light up the whole sky like that, especially the "big sky" of Montana.

The mountains were capped with snow and the moon lit up the snowy tops. It would have been a classic backdrop to the carol "Silent Night." In fact, Juliet was humming that song as she drove in silence. Her boys weren't paying any attention to the night outside. They had their ears filled with headphones from their iPods and mp3 players. Despite their presence in the car, Juliet felt very alone.

These teenage boys of hers sometimes seemed

like such strangers to her. With their big man-feet and their deepening voices, Juliet marveled at them and yet found herself feeling the gulf between her and them widen like a canyon with water raging between the land, between her feet and theirs.

Once, she had been the wife of their father, but he had been an unhappy husband and had sought out and found another life. Though she had decided to share custody with him, it was a fact that she did not trust him or feel like she had any real support from him when it came to parenting these man-children, who sometimes looked too much like him in his softer, better years, something that made her heart feel a strange, unnamable sorrow.

How she was going to manage was always on Juliet's mind. Her precious daughter was in college and about to be married. Her mother was ailing. Her new job duties loomed large at the office, with her moody, unpredictable boss always hacking away at Juliet's work and self-esteem like an unsatisfied beaver mowing through a pile of brush. Just last month Juliet had fought off wolves at the door who were threatening to shut off her power and electricity. On top of that, she had her goal of raising the boys into nice men who would do right by their wives and children. The bad economy was also looming, and she couldn't forget all the lurking headlines about the doom of the world in only a "few short years." Mayan calendars and Nostradamus Affects notwithstanding, Juliet still had to get them through it all, pay the bills, and make sure there was food in the fridge and warm coats for them to wear.

There was something that Juliet felt bewildered by. There was all this pressure of trying to survive just everyday life and get by, but then top that with wondering if she really did need to start canning and saving her bacon grease for lye soap because the economy was supposed to be so bad, and if she would indeed have any vegetables to can or bacon grease to save if things got as bad as everyone was postulating. And she wondered if the powers that be in the world were upset because of the new black president and had decided to blame all the mess the former president had made on the black president, and she asked herself whether or not he really was a socialist and what that meant.

The list went on and on. Juliet's shoulders and heart sagged and staggered from all the weight. It bore down on her as if she were a tiny Atlas trying her best to hold up a world that was getting heavier and heavier.

She decided to turn off the highway and take a country route. The only noise she had heard from her sons in the backseat was their questioning in protest as she turned onto the unfamiliar road. "Awww, is this going to take longer?"

She reassured them it wouldn't take long and that she just wanted to experience the night away from the lights of the oncoming traffic and have an easier drive home. They were candid in their disgust, but then, they usually were.

The connecting road from the highway to the road she wanted to take was unpaved. In the summer the cars driving on it left clouds of dust, but tonight even the dust was silent. She crept over it slowly, ever vigilant of how much her tires had cost her and how much farther they needed to carry her and her boys before she would have the money to replace them again.

She turned south onto the paved road and began a smooth, silent transit down the carless road. *It's probably a nice crossing for some gigantic buck deer with antlers as big across as my windshield,* she thought, keeping her eyes vigilantly on the sides of the road to watch for one of the flighty animals, who had struck two of her previous cars. She drove like this for a few minutes and noticed the stress in her hands on the wheel and the line that seemed to connect her arms across her shoulders tightening in that old familiar tension she always got. *Even a damned moonlit drive makes me tense,* she thought. She shook her head in amazement. "Always on the lookout for disaster," she said to herself. She could have said whatever she wanted since no one was listening anyway.

What utter nonsense it all seemed. Her thoughts weren't compatible with the cool beauty she was trying to experience in the night. The other thing she noticed was that the latte she'd bought at the mall had all of a sudden caught up to her and she needed to pee. She decided that since the road was dark and quiet, she could at least make the last half of her trip a little more comfortable by slipping out by the side of the road to go. She slowed the car and pulled over. The boys came out of their drummed-in ears and complained in question form, "Why are we stopping?"

"Because I have to go," she said. "It will just take a minute." She grabbed her emergency roll of tissue from the glove box and jumped out of the car.

She stayed close to the side of the car. She had to laugh at herself. Being an avid coffee drinker and someone who travelled by herself a lot, she had learned the art of being a woman who could pee by the side of the road with a certain panache. It was something she always got teased about. Once certain of no oncoming traffic, she quickly unzipped her pants and hunkered down by the side of the car, facing into the dark of the barrow pit.

A woman had a lot to do when she decided to pee outside. She needed to tuck her shirt up and carefully arrange the back of her pants so they didn't get wet. Not to mention being willing to bare a part of her that just didn't see a lot of sunshine or, in this case, moonshine, to begin with ... at least not in Juliet's case. She hadn't even worn a bikini or a real bathing suit in public in years.

Once everything was in place and ready, Juliet allowed her body to relax enough to let go of the recycled coffee. Unconsciously, while her body completed the task, she stared off into the darkness, still listening for any sounds of oncoming traffic, which would mean she might have to risk them seeing the "full moon" of her bottom on this night when there was only the bright sliver of the real one in the sky. It was a risk she would have to take, though, and she thought, "I'm already too far into the mission to stop."

But just as she was about to be done with her business, she was startled by a rustle in the grass in the barrow pit. Her first thought was that some small animal was darting about and she needn't be concerned. She'd finished and risen to pull her jeans up when she noticed something that startled her again. She backed up against the car. Her eyes began to send messages to her mind to comprehend the alarming thing that was taking shape in front of her.

There in the silvery cold night in the barrow pit next to the road was something white and shiny and fairly large. At first she thought a clump of snow was taking a strange shape and her mind was playing tricks on her. But the white, shiny lump was moving.

In the first instant, Juliet wanted to run back into the car and drive away. But Juliet, who actually was a crisis worker in her professional life, somehow allowed her practice in the art of dealing with stress to take over, or maybe it was her curiosity. What if it was a person or an animal that needed help?

Once her mind got over the hump of being

afraid, she moved on to caution. She peered into the barrow pit a little more. Her eyes were adjusting well to the darkness lit up by the sky. She watched for a moment or two as the shape shifted and moved. An animal, she thought, a deer who'd been hit by another car, poor thing. She began to dismiss it with thoughts of how, since it wasn't lying in the road to hamper other traffic, there was nothing to be done for it but to leave it and let nature take its course. In cold like this, it wouldn't last long anyway.

She began to step back and return to the car. But then the shape moved again and seemed to turn over. What Juliet saw made her give a little wild scream. The thing was now looking right at her.

For a frozen moment on that frozen night, the woman and the thing in the barrow pit stared at each other. Her senses were taking notes in fast succession: The thing in the ditch is moving; it is rising up a little; the thing is looking up at me; it has the head of a human, shoulders, hair; it's smallish, white, a child? Is it a child? Where's my cellphone? The eyes are odd; they are blue; why is it that I can see the eyes so clearly in the dark? What is that strange lump on the thing's shoulder? Should I get in the car and get safe at least? What the ... ?

By this time, the boys had come out of their mp3 trances and were starting to look out the window. Her older son, Sean, began to open the car door. Juliet didn't mean to shout, but she ordered him back in the car. She continued to stare at the thing ... then she managed to peel her eyes away from it and call to Sean again. "Sean, call 911. I think it's hurt." She saw the concern and understanding in his eyes. She noted that he was rising from his seat to get her phone from where it was perched in the little spot the car manufacturer had reserved for cellphones on the dashboard.

Something of her earlier fright dwindled enough for her to step gingerly onto the edge of the barrow pit. Her younger son, Jude, was out of the car and asking if she was okay. "I'm okay, Jude, but there is someone in the ditch who needs help ... I think."

"Mom! I can't find the cellphone!" Sean hollered. But Juliet didn't answer. She was intent on trying to approach the thing on the ground to determine what to do next with him ... her? She didn't know if it was a male or a female. "Hello?" she said. "Can you hear me?" Her thoughts skipped subjects quickly, landing on, *Oh my God, when am I going to recertify in first aid? I wonder if I remember enough to help.*

By this time, Sean had come around the hood of the car with the cellphone. Juliet questioned herself silently about whether or not either of the boys should be out of the car, but they were already standing by her. Sean held out the cellphone to her.

She was aware of Sean being so near to his full adulthood in this moment. He was tall and standing there with such concern. The light of the

Clinging to the Edge

night caught the newly born stubble on his chin and there was an assurance about him that was also new. She would have pondered this more, but there were other things to be dealt with at the moment.

"I don't know what the problem is," said Juliet. "I don't know if we should help or just call 911." She silently chided herself for being unable to decide. *Stop being ridiculous and figure this out*, and as she thought this, she decided to charge forward and told Sean to dial 911. As she was giving him instructions, she touched the little bundle lying on the ground. For as cold as it was outside, the skin seemed oddly warm. *Must've just happened*, she thought abstractedly as she checked for a pulse or anything that might tell her what this was.

"Mom, what do I tell them? They want to know what our emergency is." Sean was trying to speak to the dispatcher. Juliet was in the middle of saying, "Tell them we need assistance on Mittower Road—" when she saw something that made her stop in the middle of her sentence. It was an odd, robe-like garment wrapped around the body. It was sort of sheer and delicate. Juliet ventured to put her face close to that of the being's and was just about to put her hand under the head when she looked directly into the eyes once more ... she started again and gave another little shriek ... behind her Sean was asking her questions: "They want to know exactly where on Mittower, Mom. What do you want me to say?" And then his voice trailed off because he had suddenly noticed what Juliet had. That the thing they were trying to help was not a person or an animal at all. The moment caused them both to be silent.

Juliet was staring into its face. It's eyes held hers. They were blue like she'd seen, but not eyes like one sees with ... . They looked like small images of ... the planet earth from space? They appeared to be dark blue with swirling clouds inside them. Juliet was too stunned to find this ridiculous at that moment. The hair was silky white and curly. The skin was porcelain white but not cold to the touch; the same with the hands. The garment that clung to the small body was very light, like nothing Juliet had ever seen before. It wasn't cotton, it wasn't silk, but it was air-like and soft.

A little voice from the cellphone continued to ask questions that neither Juliet or Sean were responding to. By now, Jude had crept up behind Sean and was peering over his shoulder in wide-eyed astoundment. Juliet ventured to lift the little body up in her arms. It weighed ... nothing. How could that be? It had very definitely made noise in the barrow pit as it was shifting and turning; otherwise, it would not have caught Juliet's attention. She brought it to the boys ... and the three of them peered into its face with their hearts beating and their gazes stuck to it. The face stared back at them. The clothing was a mess, tangled about the little body like a spider's web.

Suddenly, they became aware of the dispatcher's desperate micro voice coming through to them. "Hello? Are you alright?" the voice asked.

Juliet had herself together enough that she took the phone from Sean. "Hello, this is Juliet Ramirez," she said without really thinking about why she would say such a thing. She then said, "I'm here on Mittower Road outside of Victor and I stopped by the side of the road for a minute. There is a dead animal on the side of the road that frightened me when I got out of the car because I thought it was something else. We're okay and we don't need assistance. I'm sorry I bothered you with a call ... please forgive me." The boys gasped a little at her obvious extension of the truth about the situation. And then, again without really thinking about why she did it, she hung up.

Something about the way its body was tangled in its garment and the way the little face gazed back at them had the three of them mesmerized.

Finally, Jude spoke. "What is it?"

"I don't know," Juliet whispered back. She began to gingerly pick at the flimsy, weightless material surrounding it. It reminded her of butterfly wings and was just about as fragile. She knelt on the ground and the little body shifted to adjust to Juliet's position. All the time, its wordless eyes gazing intently at her and the boys.

The longer they stared, the more intently the face stared back. Juliet ever so gently kept fidgeting with the garment until part of it was freed.

The boys leaned one each over her shoulders in rapt attention. She could feel their warm bodies on either side of her, like when they were small and she would nap with them in the warm, secure days before their world had been torn apart.

Suddenly, as if reading her brief thought, the little hand of the small being reached to touch her face. At first Juliet felt a twinge of maternal longing, but then another feeling began to warm her, one that felt faintly familiar. An answer, a completeness, a moment.

The boys noticed the answer and were exclaiming under their breath in tones of admiration, "Ohhh." Nimbly and without stopping, Juliet kept unwinding the garment with a tug here and there, until it seemed sufficiently unwound.

Gingerly, Jude reached out and touched the hair. "It's so soft," was all he said, and Sean did the same. Juliet raised the little body up as it continued its numinous gaze in their direction. It didn't seem to have feet. The trio was too astounded to ask questions yet.

Suddenly, Juliet noticed that the silver moonlight seemed even more aglow. She noticed the soft night around them and the chill and sparkle of the earth. She unwittingly pressed the little body into hers as if it were cold and needed warmth, but what she began to feel was warm and aware and something else that she hadn't felt in many long months.

The boys instinctively crowded closer her, each

now freely and gently touching the little being, as if instinctively wanting to get closer to it.

With slow, un-frightened acknowledgement, each began to hear soft, soft music. Juliet looked around to see if one of the mp3 players was hanging from one of the boys' necks but realized that the sound they were hearing was not the usual sharp noise of what the boys liked to listen to. No pounding rhythms of AC/DC or Three Days Grace. But something ancient and light and oddly wordless but filled with sounds and meaning.

It seemed to come from the earth upward and to somehow start in the body of the little being that lay in her arms. The boys were noticing it too, but no one spoke.

And although no one spoke, there were suddenly voices all around them. It was easy to startle at this, and Juliet felt the instantaneous sharp pain of fear, for they appeared from nowhere and everywhere at once. The little being raised its hand again and placed it over Juliet's heart. It gazed at Sean and Jude and they calmed. Without it saying word but from it they all heard, "Do not be afraid; for behold, I proclaim to you good news of great joy that will be for all people, for today in the City of David a savior has been born for you who is Messiah and Lord." (Luke 2:10)

And, suddenly, it was as if the light of the moon expanded. Like a tiny flame lighting up a huge space, the silvery moon lit up and domed the blue night. The sky was filled with more sparkling crystals, which appeared to drift about the mother and her sons as if it were snowing, but it was not snowing. Each tiny crystal was a prism of color.

Dancing upon the mountaintops in sheer joy were multitudes of these same creatures. Some larger and some smaller. The stars in the sky seemed to burst and explode into hundreds of beautiful creatures, like the one that lay in Juliet's arms.

It was like a giant laser show at one of those IMAX theaters, only … better … and … real.

For a few brief seconds, or possibly hours, who knew, the little family stood in that space and said nothing, too dumbstruck and fascinated to respond aloud.

The months of anxiety and sadness that had lain on Juliet's shoulders lifted. The look on her boys' faces reminded her of when they were newborns and they would gaze up into her face in fascination and absorption and even adoration. Even the subtle aches and pains that she was beginning to notice lately in her back and her knees seemed to fade. Her overdrawn checkbook, her heavy workload, her cranky ex-husband, her cares … all lifted on the air and were swept away by the dancers and the light. Her sons were close; she was strangely aware of their very souls. It was an affecting moment.

The small creature lifted itself, and Juliet felt her body give way for its movement in that simple unquestioning way that women have about such things, that acceptance, that openness: like when opening their arms to hug or their bodies for pleasure or childbirth or their hearts for letting go.

The little being floated in front of them, its little garment of faceted color and light now spread in the shape of wings, in a sort of diaphanous flow. It was small and seemed young but at the same time old and sage. It touched each boy's head lightly with the wisdom of its ageless soul.

Then it joined the others.

Minutes or years passed; who knew in that space and time? Who cared? But as peacefully as the whole spectacle had begun, it ended.

And all that was left was Juliet and her sons sitting by the side of the road, next to their car, in the moonlight on that now silent night.

None of them moved for a time.

Unbeknownst to the well-meaning sheriff's officer who pulled up soon after was that he was actually wrecking an unusual quiet and peaceful, wordless buzz. He stepped out of the car and shined his flashlight in the direction of the car and the little trio on the side of the road. "Are you alright, ma'am?" He had hold of the rectangular radio box on his shoulder and was almost at the same time speaking code into it.

A rather dazed Juliet stood, using Jude's shoulder for support, the odd ache in her back returning a little. "It's alright, Officer," was all she managed to say.

The sharp-hatted deputy shined the light all

over and said, "Dispatch said your call cut off. We just wanted to make sure there are no problems."

Juliet and the deputy recognized each other at that point. It was a small town and their paths had crossed in their work. "Oh, Sam, it's me, Juliet Ramirez. I'm sorry to have bothered you. But everything is fine. We just thought we saw ..." Her words trailed off toward the sky. What could she say that wouldn't sound like she had made a prank call?

The officer pushed his hat back a little from his head to look at her. Then he shined a light in the barrow pit. In it lay a deer that had been hit by something. Its white rump lay exposed to the road and its body was a dead torment of tangled limbs and dark little hooves. "Did you hit it, Juliet?" Deputy Sam asked.

"No. Actually, I stopped to go to the bathroom and ... uh ... I guess I couldn't tell what it was." She was answering without thinking.

Right about then, the officer shined his light on the little roll of white toilet paper and the noticeably dark trail of wetness where she'd managed to go.

"These young fellas belong to you?" the deputy said between speaking code words into the little box and a static-filled voice responding.

"Yes," said Juliet, "they are my sons, Jude and Sean."

The deputy shined the light into the car and back at Juliet, though not in her face or with any rudeness, just as a matter of making sure everything was as it should be.

"I'm sorry, Sam. I shouldn't have called; I overreacted when I thought I saw ... while I was relieving myself." She was stammering a bit. The words felt like they weren't being formed by her mouth.

"Well, when we get interrupted calls, we still try to check it out just to be sure," he went on. By now Juliet could see his white teeth smiling.

"Of course," she said. "We appreciate it very much, don't we, boys?" The boys just nodded in agreement.

"Say, Juliet, your license tabs are expired," Sam said as he shined the light on her license plate. "You shouldn't be driving like that. You'll get a ticket." Juliet was well aware of this, but she promised to get it taken care of the next day, with her overdrawn checkbook, she guessed, her pragmatic self beginning to reemerge.

Without any further words, Juliet and the boys moved to the doors of the car and began to get in. The officer seemed content that everything was alright and wasn't threatening to take her in on account of being crazy or anything, so without further ado, Juliet started her car and began to drive in the opposite direction of the deputy.

The boys didn't say a word the rest of the way home. Their headphones lay tossed on the seats next to them.

Still without speaking, they watched as the garage door automatically opened at the push of the button inside the car. No one said a word as packages and groceries were unloaded.

Teeth were brushed, pajamas put on. Juliet began to contemplate what to say to them.

As she sat on her bed brushing her hair, she lay back on the pillows for a moment. From outside in the dark hall, Jude appeared. Without saying a word, he came and lay down beside her with his head on her shoulder. Sean soon followed suit. Juliet reached up and turned out the light.

"I have no idea," was all she said. The moment in the darkness gave their eyes time to adjust. Juliet reached up her arms and tucked each boy's head onto her shoulders. She was a little surprised they didn't object.

"Were those … angels?" Jude whispered.

"Maybe," Juliet responded just as quietly. Then she turned her head a little toward him. "What do you think?"

There was more silence, and then quietly and with hesitation he said, "Yes."

Sean shifted to turn toward her, a little awkwardly since the regular-sized mattress was really too small for the three of them. He said, "Just like in the Bible."

"Yeah, I think so too," said Juliet.

"Remember the sermon the other day at Christmas Mass?" Sean said.

"Yes." Juliet hadn't realized he had listened. She'd only noticed him trying to knuckle punch his little brother's hand before she'd decided to sit between them.

He continued, "About leaving room in your heart for people in need, like the innkeeper? About giving other people hope by giving whatever you have?" The other two were silent in their acknowledgement. Sean continued to whisper. "Maybe the little angel guy was trying to tell us to have hope. Maybe we needed the hope this time."

"Maybe we did," was all Juliet responded. She pulled her growing boys to her more snugly and neither resisted. They easily dwarfed her these days. She held them tight, these strange man-children. They didn't resist or act embarrassed or question themselves about being teenagers and snuggling beside their small mother in the bed. Juliet just kept holding them, pulling them back from the other side of that deep, chasmic canyon.

Clinging to the Edge

HARRIET SAT ON THE EDGE OF HER BED, HEAD IN HER hands, elbows digging into her knees. She looked up, her fingers making jail bars around her eyes and face. The pill bottle was on the nightstand. When she had gone to see the sympathetic female doctor with the sweet face, she had received the prescription.

"These will help you relax, Harriet, so you can get some sleep. Part of your feeling blue and out of sorts lately is due to irregular sleep." So now Harriet gazed at the bottle. She had been having a hard time sleeping. The doctor had chided her, "Harriet, you're one of those women who take care of and worry about everybody but themselves. You can't let everything pile up on you at three in the morning and not go back to sleep." Then she had explained the dosage to Harriet: "These pills are just ten milligrams each, so you can decide if one is enough or if you need two to make you drowsy. Sometimes, just take one, wait an hour or so, and if you're still feeling tense, you could take another. These are just to help you relax. They are an old-fashioned antidepressant. These days, they are mostly used for insomnia and muscle relaxants. Take care of yourself, Harriet, and get some rest."

As Harriet filled the prescription, she hummed the tune to an old Rolling Stones song: "Mother needs something today to calm her down, and though she's not really ill, there's a little yellow pill ..." She tossed the pharmacy packet into the cart containing a tower of diapers, wipes, and gallons and gallons of cold, white milk. There wasn't any money in the budget for a bottle of cheap wine. So that wasn't even considered. At least there was insurance to pay for the little pills. *We manage how we must.*

In her bedroom Harriet sat alone and miserable. Inside her was a raving inferno. She was about to explode, at least she wished she could; she was desperate. If only she could just *poof* and explode into tiny pieces, she would. She couldn't think straight. Couldn't think of what to do.

Besides slap the ever-living shit out of Bob.

She poured a glass of champagne from the "anniversary" bottle Bob had brought home earlier that day. The fizzy, dancing bubbles seemed to giggle at her as they made their jolly little paths up the inside of the glass. There was no way in hell

Harriet was going to celebrate anything with that bastard tonight.

She turned on her CD player. It was Amy Grant. Amy was a musical siren who sang gospel rock, and usually she could calm Harriet, help reassure her and sing her back into having faith. But today even Amy was on Harriet's list. *Shut up, Amy.* Harriet clicked off the music and looked again at the pills and champagne. She picked up the bottle of pills. A label warning screamed at her: Do Not Drink Alcohol When Taking this Medication! Do Not Increase the Dosage Without First Contacting Your Physician! Harriet knew that these "little yellow pills" could be fatal if too large a dose was ingested. Well, she didn't want to do anything fatal … did she? She did want to calm down, and fast. *I need to get out of my head*, she thought. *I'd like to take a vacation from me.* She counted out the pills in her hand as they dropped from the bottle. One, two, three, four, five … stop there? No, six, seven, eight, nine, ten? Oh, what the hell! Eleven, twelve, thirteen … empty! *Well, you know what they say about thirteen.* She held them all in her hand. They were smoother than pebbles and chalky. *I wonder just how many too many would be*, she wondered. Then she paid attention to how quickly her heart was racing and how wrathful she felt. *Yup, might need more than a few.*

Bob was out in the living room, where he slept every night these days. He was watching *Letterman*. She could hear the "Top Ten" blaring. "Top Ten reasons Harriet went crazy!" She shook her head with a sardonic half-smile and put three pills back in the bottle. She tossed pill number ten and nine into her mouth, followed by a liberal swig of champagne. She could still hear Dave's voice; he was counting down to number eight, so she tossed two more pills in, punctuated by the champagne. *Oh shit! He's already down to five. I'd better hurry!* More pills, followed by a large gulp of champagne. She puckered her face, noting that it really wasn't very good champagne. Too cheap, of course. Why would Bob go for better?

"And now ... the number one reason why Harriet went crazy ..." Damn, Dave was in a rush tonight! She popped the rest in her mouth and finished the glass. She could hear the TV crowd roaring with laughter and applause. "Good job, Harriet! You've done it!" Their laughter swirled around her and she could imagine Dave's very wry face peering through his silver-rimmed glasses while Paul Shaffer played that old, skippy cancan dance theme. The trumpets were resonant with the rhythmic clapping of the audience. She lay down. Her thoughts racing, her heart still beating furiously inside her ribcage.

It had been a crummy week; well, a few too many crummy weeks in a row actually. And today, today had been the crown jewel turd of bad days. The absolute shits. She and a coworker, Ellen, had been putting together trial exhibit notebooks. In the course of the conversation, Ellen had used the term "emotionally labile" to describe a cranky client. It was a term new to Harriett, so she tried to say it out loud but couldn't pronounce it. Ellen said, "Just think of the word 'labia'. It sounds a lot like that." Both of the women snickered. Then it had become a crude joke throughout that workday. Every time one of them got a little edgy, the other one would say, "Now don't get labile; keep your cool!" and they would both laugh. At one point, another coworker had unloaded on Harriet. Ellen had said in the most persnickety voice she could parrot, "Well, she's a bit labile today." Saying the word had provided a little sanity. Funny because the word referred to mood swings, instability, and anything but sanity.

At noon, Ellen and Harriet had lunch together. The two women knew each other pretty well. They had worked together five years now. "What the hell was up with plane tickets you ordered for Ted?" Harriet had asked as they ate.

Ellen rolled her eyes. "Well, he asked me to order two tickets, one to Maui and the other to Indiana."

"Really?" Harriet's eyebrows furrowed.

"Yes, and then Ted's wife called to say she was going to come and pick up her ticket to Indiana. I asked if she wanted Ted's too. Well, she didn't seem to know what I was talking about, so when I got off the phone, I asked Ted if he wanted me to give her his ticket as well. Well, Harriet, you should have seen the look on his face. His eyes got all big and wide, and he got all pissy acting with me and said, 'You didn't tell her about the Maui ticket, did you?' and I said, 'No, because she seemed confused.' And then he got up and shut his door and then ..." Ellen took a deep breath and shook her head, unable to say more.

"What is it, Ellen?" Harriet encouraged.

"Well, he told me I must not tell her, that it was a surprise and that ... well, that it would be a detriment to his marriage as well as my job if she were to find out. Then he told me that when she came to pick up the ticket that I was to tell her I'd made a mistake and the other ticket was for someone else in the office. Oh yes, and then told me to order a dozen red roses and have them sent to an address in Seattle this afternoon.

Harriet stopped eating. "That rat bastard is having an affair, isn't he?"

Ellen nodded her head. "That's what I think, Harriet, because when I thought about the dates on the tickets, they are for the same dates. Ted's mother-in-law lives in Indiana. So while she is visiting her mother, Ted is going to be in Maui with ... Miss Seattle, I guess." The women looked at each other in disgust.

Ted Obering was the chief associate of the firm. He was a big, ugly man with a balding head and a potbelly. Of particular disgust to Harriet was the large, flesh-colored mole on the side of his nose. Absolutely gross. Why he'd never had it removed was beyond her. It wasn't that he couldn't afford the removal cost.

Harriet said, "You know, I can't even imagine his own wife sleeping with him. I really can't imagine anyone else wanting to either. Gack!"

Ellen began to giggle. "I wonder if he's as dense about screwing as he is about how he treats us?"

Harriet's food soured in her mouth. Really, *who would* want to do it with that mole? "Well, did Mrs. Obering come in for the ticket?" she asked.

"Yes, she did. And I lied to her. I took the heat; I told her I'd made a mistake. You know, I don't like her; she's a raving bitch, but having to lie for him was just so ..." Ellen broke off and added quietly, "I can't lose this job."

Harriet was furious. She tried to be comforting. "Well, Ellen, you did what you had to. He left you no choice. I'm sorry." And then she tried to say brightly, "Maybe he's just going surfing. I mean, can't you just see him on a surfboard trying to catch a few waves? The lifeguards would think he was a whale swimming inland, or better yet, a shark! And then they would start blowing whistles and yelling for everyone to get out of the water. People would be running for the beach screaming, 'Shark, shark!' and, in a way, since he's an attorney ..."

Ellen was laughing along with Harriet. Their laughter was high and sharp, like hens after laying eggs. "Harriet, I don't know what I'd do without you."

"Well, who knows what he's up to? We really don't know for sure. The flowers might be for a sick aunt."

Ellen looked directly at Harriet. "Get real, Harriet."

The two had paid for their meals and were walking down the street with Harriet's umbrella haloed over them as the gray rain fell. They had on knee-length, parka-style coats tied with loopy belts around their middles. They each wore dark stockings that melted into dark shoes. Their feminine feet made little click-tap, click-tap sounds on the concrete. They stopped to window shop. In a store window, there was a display of diaphanous lingerie draped on silk hangers. Both contemplated for a moment. "Bob still sleeping on the couch?" asked Ellen as they stared through the glass. Harriet gave a silent little nod while she thought about how she was still carrying around twenty pounds of "baby fat" left over from being pregnant with Joey. All this lingerie would look ridiculous on her. "Harriet, you always make me feel better when I'm feeling low. Sometimes I worry you don't get enough of that same medicine from others ... Bob, me. I'm here if you need me."

Harriet was touched by Ellen's insight. "Thanks, Ellen. I appreciate it." The two walked on.

"You should haul Bob's butt to a marriage counselor," Ellen commented.

"Yeah, I know."

Harriet had left the office that afternoon determined to put all the office baggage behind her. It was her and Bob's anniversary and a Friday. Perhaps he would take her out to dinner and they would have a chance to talk, maybe even come to some sort of understanding. Maybe she could even talk him into marriage counseling. *I could still get a sitter for the evening*, she thought, *if he would ask me to.* Then she began to daydream about sitting in front of a would-be counselor. The counselor would look over the two young married people with a knowledgeable air and ask, "What seems to be the problem, kids?" And Harriet would say, "Well, to be frank, Counselor, this man is my oldest child. He's as big a kid as our preschool-age boys are. He is a very poorly behaved kid at that. And I'm jealous of this blonde at his office that is childless and still has a waistline and wears push-up bras—not because she needs them; she just wears them. She hasn't breastfed two kids, so her boobs still point upward. He mentions her sometimes, and she's a little too sweet to me when I call him at the office. And the shit I could tell you that he has pulled … . He went fishing two weeks after Joey was born. I tried to understand, really I did, but it was a bad time for him to go. Really, you'd give me an award for putting up with him for ten years. You will want to pull a ruler out of your desk drawer and rap his knuckles, hard! I know you will tell him to start behaving or else you'll come after him yourself, with a bigger ruler. Then I'm sure everything will be just fine! He'll be ever so much better and you'll have fixed us. We may name our next child after you we'll be so grateful." These thoughts made Harriet laugh and then she began to cry. She pulled into the driveway of the daycare and wiped her eyes. She looked at herself in the rearview mirror and said, "Harriet, pull it together, girl. Stop being so labile!"

She was excited to see her boys. She always was. She had been trying to figure out a way to work part-time and stay home with them more. It could happen ... if Bob would support it and agree. Perhaps if they budgeted more carefully, if they cut up some credit cards. The little boys had cried when she had dropped them off at daycare that morning. "We don't want you to go, Mommy! We hate daycare." Ryan, the oldest, had wailed while Joey, the youngest, had hung on her leg like a koala bear on a branch. Ryan continued to whimper even after the caregiver had plied him with a couple of his favorite toys. Now, at the end of the day, Harriet walked into the room where the boys were playing with other kids their ages. They looked at her and began to cry. "Mommy, Mommy, we don't want to go home! We're playing. We hate going home!"

Harriet wrangled them both into their coats and car seats amid their protests. It wore her out. It made her crabby. As if to prolong her black frame of mind, the boys had cried all the way home from daycare and the wonderful Missoula traffic had been even more constipated than ever. Finally reaching home, she checked the mail and lugged the boys in from the car one at a time. Joey was asleep and she couldn't get him to wake up.

He'd never go to bed tonight if he took a nap now. Ryan was hyperactively inserting the Nintendo cartridge into the slot. "Donkey Kong! Donkey Kong! Donkey Kong!" he yelled over and over.

Harriet looked over the pile of spilt mail as she picked it up from the front step, where she'd dropped it. A feeling of dread dropped into her stomach as she picked out was she knew was a special notice from the bank. She opened it viciously, making ragged edges of the envelope. Five bounced checks at a twenty-dollar service charge each. There was a note enclosed. Harriet read it and heard the undertone of the letter: "You're a loser! Get your ass in gear or get it out of here! You're a miserable failure of a woman!" It was even signed in ink by a bank employee and not just a computer. Bad checks. *Hell!* thought Harriet. *If it weren't for bad checks. I'm not sure this family could survive.* She blinked back tears. One of the checks was to the grocery store, two others were for gas, and the other two were some doings of Bob's. Every paycheck seemed to be spent before it could be placed in her hand. More tears surfaced and more tears were held back. *No anniversary dinner for us,* she thought as she shoved the notice under a pile of more bills.

She had forgotten to take anything out for dinner, so she pulled last night's stew out of the fridge. It had tasted terrible last night; it would taste even worse tonight. She put it on the stove to warm. Just then, she heard Ryan yell from the bathroom, "MOOOOOMMMYYY, wipe my butt off!" She ran to the bathroom. He had taken all of the toilet paper off the roll and stuck most of it in the toilet. He had also attempted to flush the toilet. There was shitty water and toilet paper goop flowing over the edge of the porcelain rim. Harriet attempted to clean Ryan's behind with what dry toilet paper was left. There were slimy little turds everywhere. "Ryan! What did you do this for? Don't be messing with the toilet paper! And don't flush. I'll do that. See the big mess you've made?"

Ryan was very interested in the mess, he said, "Look, Mom! A poop! It's brown, just like a bear. Bear and brown begin with 'B'!"

Harriet thought, *The kid is a frickin' genius, but he can't wipe his own butt!* But to the child, she said, "Damn it, Ryan, get the hell out of here and let me clean this crap up!" Ryan's eyes got very big at the tone of her voice; she usually liked it when he could name letters. "Wait!" said Harriet. "Give me your socks, they're wet!" Roughly, she yanked the socks from his feet, and then she practically threw him out in the hallway.

Undeterred by her crankiness, he ran back into the living room, shouting rhythmically, "Dammit, dammit, dammit!" It was a new word. He loved new words. The noise woke Joey, who began to bawl vigorously. The squalling noise filled the air and bounced off the walls.

Then the fire alarm went off.

Ryan began to shriek and covered his ears.

Harriet went sliding out to the hall, where she noticed a gray, foul-smelling smoke beginning to curl its way throughout the kitchen. She sprinted to the stove; the flames gave the kitchen a strange and shadowy glow as they joyously consumed the leftover stew.

"Mom! Fire!" Ryan yelled over the cacophony of Joey's crying and the fire alarm. "Stop, drop, and roll!" he shouted over and over again. He tried to get the bemused Joey to join in the routine, but instead just managed to piss Joey off. He coldcocked Ryan in the chin. Ryan began to sob, "Mommy! He hit me!" Then he hit Joey back, and they fell to the ground, a blob of chubby little boy fists and anger.

Well, at least they are dropping and rolling, Harriet thought as she grabbed the baking soda. The happy, mocking flames were extinguished. She grabbed the pan with a pot holder and flung them both out of the patio door to the backyard. She watched numbly as the pan flipped like a clumsy Frisbee and hit with a thunk on the ground. The phone rang. "What!" she shouted into it. It was Bob. He sounded so jolly. How dare he? The world inside the house was still a rage. "Get your ass home! Now!" She was shaking and slammed the phone down.

She began screaming. Wildly. Had Harriet become crazy in that moment or had craziness become Harriet? She began to feel consumed with a black ugliness as she gave in to the rage. She let it vomit out of her lungs, her fingers, her soul, her stomach, her heart, her nose, and her mouth. It streamed from everywhere inside her.

And then silence.

Even the fire alarm had somehow ceased to buzz. It gave out weak, pathetic little chirping sounds, a signal the battery was running out. *How prophetic*, Harriet thought. The boys had stopped their wrestling and stared at her with their little pink mouths open wide. *That's it; it's over*, thought Harriet. The batteries are dead.

Harriet washed her hands and made the boys peanut butter sandwiches. She put their milk in little cups with lids so they couldn't spill it as easily. She thought of how her mother would have chastised her about giving the kids peanut butter for dinner. "Oh, what the hell. Protein is protein," she consoled herself. She began to clean up the mess in the bathroom, which was just plain icky. She hauled out a large bottle of bleach and poured some in a bucket. She splashed some of the bleach on her skirt. She hadn't even thought about changing out of her work clothes. She looked at her ruined garment and cursed to herself. She continued to scrub the floor and the toilet. She looked up at her reflection in a full-length mirror. She had been beautiful once. Now she was tired and puffy and had a look of cynicism that had never been there before. She got the bathroom cleaner out and decided to wash out the tub and the vanity as long as she was at it. She scrubbed hard. Even those obnoxious "scrubbing bubbles" couldn't keep up! There were tears draining out of Harriet's eyes in unnoticed rivulets. They made little plopping sounds as they hit the tub. She scrubbed those bounced checks, along with Ted Obering's crappy treatment of her friend and coworker. She scrubbed his disgusting mole off his disgusting face. She scrubbed away all traces of the overflowing toilet and its contents. She wished Bob would come home and tell her they were going away for six months to some little, obscure, warm island, just them and their two boys.

When she was done, the whole bathroom sparkled and smelled bleachy fresh. Ryan came up behind her and hugged and kissed her bottom. Harriet was short and it was the only place he could reach. He usually did it when they were in a public place, like the video store or at a checkout counter, where there were lots of people behind her. She reached around and patted his head after she removed her rubber glove. He had smeared peanut butter all over his face and now it was all over her skirt. Joey came around the corner all sticky with breadcrumbs and jelly and smelling from his dirty diaper. More poop to clean up. So she changed him.

She heard the front door open, followed by Bob calling out, "Where's my boys?" At once, the two little men raced down the hall to their dad. "Time to show you what Daddy bought you today. Come on out and see!" There were squeals of delight as they scrambled out.

For a moment, a very brief one, Harriet imagined that he had brought her something wonderful for their anniversary. Some silly thing, like a written notice to her boss saying she was quitting her bullshit job. No such luck. When she peered out the window, she saw Ryan running around a bright red, brand new, three-quarter ton pick-up truck, screaming, "A fire truck! Look, Mommy! A fire truck! It's red! Does it make a loud noise, Daddy? Huh? Does it?"

Bob was smiling like he did after he'd eaten a Little Debbie Moon Pie, his favorite. Harriet was horrified. "What the ... ?" she stopped. She still had a diaper in her hand and one plastic glove on from cleaning. Her dress was splotched with bleach and her nylons were run. Her eyes were puffy and her mascara had made little black trails down her face. The neat hairstyle she usually kept intact was all frizzy. "Happy anniversary, darlin'," said Bob all cheesy and breezy.

Harriet could only stare. "Bob, tell me you're not serious. Tell me you're joking."

Bob finally stopped with the silly grin he was exhibiting and took notice of her appearance. "Geez almighty, Harriet, you look like hell!"

Harriet could feel the anger burst forth again in renewed force. "Tell me you did not buy that truck, Bob."

Bob laughed, "Well, you need to cosign, but

Carlotta's boyfriend said you could just take the paperwork to your office for a notarization."

Harriet couldn't seem to find her breath "Carlotta? You mean that blonde *skank* at your office? Her boyfriend? What the hell are you saying?"

Bob was clueless. "Well, her boyfriend, Marcus, is a loan officer at the credit union. He gave me a great deal at a stealer interest rate." Harriet raced back into the house. For a knife? Well, it wouldn't have been impossible. Instead she grabbed the notice from the bank that she'd found that afternoon. She went back to the porch and flung that and the signed note at Bob. They flounced waywardly at his feet.

"That, my dear husband, is note from the bank! It says we are overdrawn and there is $100 worth of bad check charges. How in the hell do you think we are going to pay for a truck when we don't fucking have enough money to buy groceries? How in the hell did you get a loan with this going on?"

Bob gave her an innocent, hurt look, like she had struck him. "Don't freak out, Harriet. Marcus covered the checks with the loan. And don't swear so much in front of the boys. You know how Ryan picks everything up these days."

Just then, Ryan tugged on Bob's jacket. "Daddy, did you know a skank is black with a white stripe? We learned about them in preschool. They like to eat trash." The little guy was so justifiably proud of his knowledge. Bob glared at Harriet.

His look so infuriated Harriet that the vile

frustration began to spew from Harriet's throat, and she became as unraveled as the panty hose she was wearing. "Bob, we can't, you can't ... NO! I'm not paying for this ..."

Just then, their neighbor Rick sauntered over with two beers in hand and offered one to Bob. "Whoa, Bobby, this your new rig?"

Harriet gave Bob a stare that should have had him bleeding. But Bob just chuckled. "Hey, yeah. It's an anniversary gift, but she's telling me she don't like it!" Rick looked at Harriet in total disbelief, and then he looked twice, noticing her appearance. Embarrassed and pissed to the limit, Harriet grabbed her two boys and ran in the house.

Bob spent his evening showing off the damned red truck to anyone in the neighborhood who wanted to look. Harriet could only feel like the inside of a brooding volcano, the disgust brimming out of her silence like an evil about to engulf. Her heart felt sick thinking about how she wouldn't be able to cut her work hours back to part-time with another damned payment to make. Bob made good money, but holy crap, there still didn't to ever seem be enough. If she asked the firm if she should consider cutting her hours, they would say "not."

She scrubbed the boys clean, using Bob's bathroom, not the one she had just cleaned. After she scrubbed the boys, there was a light gray, soapy ring around the tub. She left it. Bob hated it when people didn't clean up after themselves. They were both clean freaks, but Harriet just couldn't give a shit tonight. She hoped it would make him livid.

She put the boys to bed. Usually, she loved rocking and singing to them. But tonight she could barely stand it. Joey wriggled out of her grasp, "Ow, Mommy!" She was rocking really fast and must have squeezed the poor little kid. Ryan asked for another drink of water and she snapped at him. *Oh, this is pitiful*, she thought. She immediately got him more water. She kissed Ryan frantically, "I'm sorry, baby. Mommy's just tired." Joey was already asleep and Ryan seemed to settle down. It was a partial relief to get them to bed. She was still positively choleric.

Bob had come in from outdoors without saying anything to her. *The big show must be over*, thought Harriet. He started rummaging around in the refrigerator. Harriet went into what was now "her" bedroom and closed the door. She angrily tossed the ruined hose and the skirt into the garbage. She put on her most comfortable, ugly pajamas and didn't bother to wash her face or brush her teeth. She was still seething. There was no way to talk to Bob right now without ripping his head off or waking the kids. She thought of calling Ellen to vent, but it was now nearly 10:30 in the evening, and Ellen had her own family to take care of.

Harriet went out into the kitchen and grabbed a bottle of champagne that had been forgotten; it had been purchased as a means to celebrate their anniversary. It stood all alone on the counter like an absurd groomsmen who'd been abandoned and not asked to dance. Bob was totally engrossed in watching Dave Letterman hug the long-legged bimbos that were part of each show's opening. She didn't bother to say goodnight and neither did he. She gave a brief thought to how on this very evening ten years ago, on their wedding night, they had ... well, it didn't seem real any more.

And now, there was Harriet after she'd taken the pills and swallowed the awful champagne. In her wavering state, she said aloud to no one, "Bet if I was one of Dave's bimbos or Miss Carlotta, he'd have at least gone to Costco and purchased a better bottle at discount. But, no, I only get Albertson's cheap two-for-ten deal. Jerk. See if he ever gets to sleep in this room again. Asshole."

Damn, it was taking a long time for this supposedly lethal combination to work its relaxation trick on her. "Shouldn't I be seeing bugs dance or hear colors singing? C'mon, don't I deserve at least one cheap trip?" Just then, she noticed a piece of paper sticking out from underneath the bed. It had a bright red smudgy handprint on it. Ryan had made it at daycare. Someone had written "For Mommy" on it. Then, at the bottom, it said "Ryan" and gave the date from a few days before. She held the little handprint to her cheek. She wondered if she had even taken the time to thank Ryan and praise his good work. Then it hit her. A wave of dizziness overcame her. "What the hell

Clinging to the Edge

have I done? Did I really take ten of those things? What the hell ... ?"

"Bob!" she cried out. Or did she? Because the voice she heard didn't seem to be coming from her. Oh crap. OH CRAP. *Please tell me I was just kidding. Please tell me I didn't really ...* "Bob!" There was that voice again. *Oh my God, I'm going to puke!*

Somewhere in the distance, Ryan was trying to tell her something. He'd what? Wet his pants and his blankie was wet? *No problemo! Mom will fix it, but wait ... Mom isn't moving. There is a howling in the room that sort of reminds me of a child crying ... Oh yes, Ryan, what did you need?* The howling got bigger and bigger, like when a dog hears a fire siren or when his master dies.

Now Harriet was feeling calm, and floating, just floating. Visions swirled into her head. She thought of how just last week she'd received a raise. Not much of one. She'd taken it graciously, not thinking to ask for more. She saw herself smiling at her boss. Smiling with her large, white teeth after she'd licked the silvery spoon the raise had been served on. Shit oozed between the tiny cracks of her teeth. She swallowed quickly in case he might think she was ungrateful and take it away. *I will stop being so labile.* She thought of how it was sort of funny that a word about being crazy sounded a lot like the word labia. Labia, referring to a female body part. *A labile labia. That's me. I'd better call a doctor because I don't think I'm supposed to be here. Bob will marry one of Dave's bimbos ... or*

Carlotta. *"Why do you keep mentioning Carlotta? I love you, Harriet."* Harriet could just about imagine that Bob had said that, but no, he had forgotten how.

Ryan and Joey, they were both crying now. *What is troubling them so? I'd better go and hold them.* She had to get to them! There was the smell of vomit and sweat all around her. *Oh my goodness, if I could just stop retching long enough, I would go and find them.* So much vomit, and the toilet overflowed and the stew pot boiled over; the flames spewed over onto the side.

There were lights and masked faces, strong arms everywhere, and she was brick-heavy. She couldn't get to the boys! Didn't those masks and arms know Ryan needed dry pants? All she could do was barf.

By the next evening, Harriet was foggily sitting next to a hospital bed she'd slept in all day. She was hooked to an IV dripping in to flush out the former evening's champagne and pill cocktail. The night in the emergency room had been rough, but Harriet didn't remember much. Now Bob came into the room with the boys. The boys were glad, God, so glad to see their mommy. The red lights and sirens had scared them the evening before. Bob looked scolded and sheepish as he stood around with his hands in his pockets. His eyes were on Harriet. Such a look! But he didn't seem mad. The nurse came in; she was a cheerful, bustling, busy little thing. She brought Harriet a little pill called Prozac in a little white cup. She looked at Bob and Harriet and then at the boys. "Take this, Harriet, and then, why don't I see about some ice cream for these little cuties? Give you two a chance to chat?"

The boys heard the words ice cream and were eager to find out if they could score some. They each took her hands, and she led them out, talking cheerfully. Ryan went skipping down the hall. "Mommy's sick," Ryan announced. "She barfed all over her bedroom. It really smelled!" His voice couldn't have been louder.

Bob knelt by Harriet's chair. She was still wan and puny-looking. Harriet couldn't look him in the eyes. She felt as guilty as he looked. "Some anniversary," was all she could say.

"Well, it's not like you haven't thrown up on me before. You pretty much soaked me when Joey was born. And you know you can't exactly hold your liquor." Bob tried to smile as he said this. There was silence then. Finally he said, "I returned the pickup back to the dealership."

Harriet was looking at her hands. *I feel so ashamed*, she thought. It wasn't worth any of this. *Shit, I can't even get loaded right.* She stayed silent.

"Is it Carlotta you want?" she finally said, looking straight at Bob. *Carlotta especially isn't worth all of this*, she thought, more ashamed. *Me dead over some skank? A ditzy brunette maybe, but not a blonde. Carlotta is not the issue. What the hell was I thinking?*

Bob took her hand and rubbed it over his stubbly cheek. "Harriet, I ... Carlotta is a looker, and kind of a flirt, but ... I'm not into her, I promise. She's just someone to, you know, talk to sometimes." He lay his head in her lap.

Harriet was still somewhere in the fog, clinging to the edge, a very fragile, chalky, crumbling edge. In another room, someone was listening to Regis Philbin saying, "Is that your final answer?" and she started to laugh. Then she cupped Bob's head in her hands and looked into his teary, repentant eyes. "Grow up, Bob."

He sat back on his heels, ignoring her comment. "Your doc says you need to be in here a few days. She wants you to see a counselor or a psychiatrist or something, wants to know if you're still a 'threat' to yourself ..." His voice trailed off. He was in his own fog. He didn't know what was happening. What did he know about labia?

Harriet began to chuckle ironically. "I'm definitely a threat. Lock me up; really, a few days of being asked about the voices in my head and having my urine tested are just what I need. Maybe I can do some copywriting for a new Prozac commercial like, 'Can't accomplish a successful attempt on your life? Well, that's okay, because all you need to do is take a pill. Pills fix everything. And when they don't, theeere's Prozac!' So, really, you and the kids go to Hawaii for the duration. Have a great time; don't worry about me." She was trying to be her old self. It wasn't working.

Bob grabbed her hands and looked directly in her eyes, not smiling. "Harriet, I'm serious. You really scared me ... and the boys." He gulped back a sob. "The doctor says you are depressed." He said the word like it was a foreign language or a bad word to be whispered where the kids couldn't hear it.

Harriet felt the loss in his comment. She felt some distant road strangely appearing in front of her, still covered in gray fog. She disentangled her hands from his. "No, Bob. I'm not depressed. I'm labile. Emotionally labile."

Joyful Oddities

THERE'S JUST SOMETHING ABOUT CEMETERIES. I LIKE them. Mystical, holy places fertilized by death—they are quiet and serene. The wind breathes a lonelier, different sound. Birds always sing solo and the trees sway more gently. There is such peace that perhaps this is what gives meaning to the phrase, "Rest in Peace." Some folks—in fact, most of the ones I know—avoid cemeteries like painful rashes. However, if I have an excuse, I go. When I was young and had time for such things, I sought out the loneliness and tranquility of our little cemetery, which sat on a pert hill just south of our tiny town.

In the summer, it was one of the most alive, yet quiet places I knew. I never told anyone of my habit of visiting the resting place of the dead. Graves were crowned with ornate, old-fashioned memorials, with stone flowers and angels bejew-eling each one. Not in existence yet were the flat, pink stones of the current day. I loved the history and mysteriousness, the sadness and, yes, even the morbidity of that place. With the echoes of the dead ringing in my ears, I would lie on the cool grass and relish the warmth of the sun splashing in dappled gold drops here and there on the fra-grant carpet of green as the bees hummed softly. Once, after making sure no one was about to see my impish irreverence, I turned a few somersaults in the summer grass over the resting places named for some unknown persons who lay underneath. I never knew just what came over me and, being kid, didn't give it much thought. Perhaps, I was as strange a child as everyone said.

Years later, I'm visiting another cemetery, located on a gentle hill filled with lovely old-fash-ioned gravestones. (The best cemeteries are always on hills.) My young sons scamper over the grass that blankets the place, which is chock-full of dead ancestors from their dad's side of the family. We are there to view the raw and recent grave of a much-loved relative.

My mind floats back to the last time I saw Edna. She was ninety years old. She was a big-boned woman, an ex–school teacher and elementary principal. She never had children of her own, just everyone else's. The smell of antiseptic permeated the convalescent home where she last resided on this earth. I was frazzled after our journey to visit her. I was thirty-five years old, holding a fussy baby and hoping and praying my toddler didn't unplug her roommate's oxygen tank. My shirt was soaked with breast milk; my hair was messy and wind-blown; my eyes, sunken pits deprived of sleep. I was a far cry from the composed elderly lady sitting across from me, learning to paint with water colors for the first time in her life. Her knitting yarns, needles, and a few books were near her wheelchair.

She was, in her proper elementary school principal fashion, cross-examining me. She was the only person in my life who had ever been able to ask nosy questions and still have my respect.

"You are keeping busy with the children and work?" she asked kindly. I replied in the affirmative, even though I was not sure if it was an observation or a question. "And are keeping up on your writing?" she asked.

I stuttered and stammered a moment and looked away like the guilty school child that has not made the proper effort with her studies. "Well, not really. I am busy with the kids and the house and ... ." I trailed off, wondering if she could possibly comprehend my daily agenda.

She kept a steady eye on me, the shrewd educator making up her mind about the student, and nodded with what I hoped was understanding. Clumsily, I offered her the only hopeful thing a lazy pupil could think of: "But I'm still interested!" I said it with a bright smile and hoped the interrogation was over. She turned back to her canvas, her weakening hands and fingers still training for something new. It was a liquid blue color she is working with. I imagined it was the color of the tear that came to the corner of my eye when she said, "You have a good mind; don't forget that." It was a simple, direct statement. Someone else may not have understood, but I felt the impact of her sage comment like a wave crashing to shore.

Edna was my husband's great-aunt, and she was beloved to me for her spry frankness. The thing about Edna was, I never had to make an effort to like her, not in the way I've tried to like other relatives that I inherited by birth or marriage, because I felt obligated to do so. Liking Edna in a genuine sense was like doing somersaults on a sunny hillside. It was just enjoyable.

The gentle wind blows over the stubbly brown grass that is waving dryly over the muddy-tan landscape of the Roberts City cemetery. My sons and I play hide and seek among the gravestones. My husband pauses at the plot that holds the earthly remains of his kin. Other than seeing Edna's name carved in a flat, pink stone, I don't feel much connection to those he is deeply remembering. Yet by having his children, I became part of those people who are only names on a stone to me. I recognize that these dead are part of the root system that gives breath and being to the two small children that now laugh and giggle as they run and peek from behind each stone.

I run freely with my little sprouts, playing the

game. Now I pause to read the name and date on a marker ... now I count to ten ... now I remember my childhood love of graveyards ... now I notice we are not alone.

I am amazingly unstartled at the sudden sight of many spirits perched on some of the gravestones. They are watching us peacefully with sublime expressions. I pass by them, and they gaze, unconcerned, unburdened, just waiting. Even a little child with plump cheeks and a dimpled chin just squints as the sun passes between my shadow and his face. Looking behind the child, on the vacant slope that has been set aside for more dead to fill it in the years to come, I catch my breath in surprised delight at what I am seeing.

The images are clad in their burial clothes, some in dark, somber colors, and others in lavenders and florals. The young and the old together, yet oddly all the same age in spirit. All are laughing noiselessly from somewhere inside themselves, and incredibly, they start somersaulting! Some do so in jubilant, raucous races, others just for the ceaseless enjoyment of doing so.

Spirits, once confined in aged or diseased, tired or wounded bodies, are now rolling head over heels in joyful motions of suppleness and freedom from worldly affliction. They have no sickness, no mortgages, no war, no sorrow, and no dinners to fix, just somersaulting because they can.

A young man in white sailor's suit and hat winks at me. His bright eyes are no color at all except that which mirrors the bright blue of the sky. He picks up the little child and hoists him up on his shoulders. The child seems nonchalantly happy as he is taken over to join the wild jubilation in front of them.

A woman sits on the stone next to where I stand. She is oddly familiar, but in the split second of the moment, I can't quite place her. She smiles at my children and then raises her hand toward mine. I feel the faintest of a soft breeze pass over my fingertips like the breath of an angel.

Almost as suddenly as I beheld this splendid sight, my young son jerks me back with a psychotic yank. His eyes are snapping like electricity because he has "found" me. For a moment, I think his eyes might mysteriously resemble something I see in a few of these rollicking souls reeling in circles on the hill. I glance back at the curious scene for another look, but they are gone. Only the inexplicable, noiseless laughter echoes in the wind.

My son and I turn and, hand in hand, return to my husband and our parked van. I look behind me once more, hoping … but nothing. I feel exhilarated, blessed to have been given such a treat! I blow a kiss toward Edna's grave and whisper, "Thank you, my sweet."

"You have a good mind; don't forget that." She had that said the last time we spoke.

Days afterward, when I tell my husband my quirky little story, he looks at me as if to say, "You've lost your mind!" Then he just grins and says, simply, "You're weird," and kisses my cheek. I laugh at his response, secure that he understands my oddities. Perhaps, I am as strange a child as everyone says.

About the Author

THERESA RIVERA GREW UP IN WESTERN MONTANA IN A RURAL community where she was expected to be a nice, Catholic girl who behaved. When that didn't happen, she became a feisty, single mom of three. She obtained her social work degree at the age of 42.

In her work, she's been privileged to walk beside a wide population of humans that include abused children and adults, grief, trauma, cancer survivors and others facing life's struggles. She has facilitated writing workshops and support groups. She has promoted journaling as a means to express oneself and to promote healing, growth and creativity to survivors. She enjoys writing about life's messes while adding her core values of faith, humor and determination. She now lives in Washington state to be close to her grandchildren and continues her work advocating for others. She enjoys her independence, hiking, camping, traveling, good wine, music, her strong ties to her family, friends and of course... journaling.

Printed in July 2019
by Rotomail Italia S.p.A., Vignate (MI) - Italy